Hyperboreans

By

David Jordan

Published by

BeulAithris
Publishing

Scotland

First Published 2023

ISBN: 9798378259014

Text © David Jordan

Cover Art © Mark Hetherington

For Willie Lynch

I

This is a story about civilisation and imagination.

The ancient Greeks knew a thing or two about these. They imagined a mythic people who lived far north of them, whom they called Hyperboreans. Many people believe that it was the Irish they were thinking of. If that is so, we shouldn't disappoint the Greek spirit, now. The spirit of the people who invented Western Civilisation. For if they were dreaming about us when they did so, then maybe we had a hand in making that Civilisation, too. And we should play our part in the renewing of it. That means ideas. That means energy. That means imagination.

And so, here goes.

I clearly remember the first comic book shop to open up in Cork. It was a small enclave in a second-hand clothes store on Winthrop Street. The name of the shop was written in chalk on a blackboard just outside the entrance: Ummagumma Rose Comics it said in large, looping white letters. This was the mid 90s and I was a couple of years out of secondary school when we discovered it. 'We' are myself and my friend and business partner, James. I had recently joined the ranks of the unemployed and James had gone on to college to study English literature.

So, the Ummagumma Rose was a major discovery for us. Prior to its opening, the only comic book you could get in Cork that resembled an American comic was the weekly anthology, *2000AD*. After so many years of deprivation, suddenly having access to Marvel and DC books was like the breaking down of a dam and the freeing of a river. Instantly, there was so much more choice! I wasn't that much interested in mainstream superhero comics like Batman, Superman and Spiderman. What interested me more were the horror titles. Anything with a 'suggested for mature readers' sign on it caught my eye. And there was one comic in particular that I really gravitated toward. Its covers were dark and disturbing and often surreal, and the artwork and stories inside lived up to them. And there wasn't a cape in sight. The book was called *John Summoner: Shot to Hell*.

Anyway, the shop lasted less than a year before it folded. That's a short period, especially when you consider it was the city's very first comic book shop, but you have to consider how small and obscure the place was. It was doomed to a short life. But it was open long enough for me to discover *Shot To Hell*, and this was the inspiration behind me and James' initial venture into occult investigation.

So, what was so great about this comic? Firstly, John Summoner was no caped vigilante. He did wear a flowing trench coat, which could be seen as a compromise but that was as far as it went. He was no superhero or science hero. His motives were perhaps the same, but he was entirely human. He was flawed. He was flawed big time. I mean he could be a total bastard. He was fucked up. He was so fucked up it was heroic. I mean he smoked and drank like a demon. He lost friends like poker chips. He gave the finger to the Devil, literally. And at his core he still managed to stay good. His heart was never up for negotiation. These days that might not be so original but back then it was totally new.

Secondly, the world in which Summoner moved and operated was different from the rest of the DC universe. It was an underworld. The underworld of a man who put on many masks: investigator, psychic, shaman, mage. Many of the characters were unreal. Summoner operated in the between zones where 'reality' was not so hard and fast. The Dreaming, cyberspace, trance induced vision quests, astral planes. He did it all. And last but not least, he had a sense of humour. *Shot To Hell* was the only comic ever to make me laugh out loud. So, now you know a bit about the comic that inspired us.

What about the business? Ah, the business. I've dedicated twenty years of my life to it. I'm still on social welfare. I get no rewards or recognition for it. I have no wife or family. I've made more enemies than friends. So, why do I do it? I'm constantly asking myself that very question and I can never come up with an answer. The truth is, I don't know. Maybe I just want to change the planet for the better. Or maybe I just want to avoid getting a regular 9-5 job. Maybe I'm idealistic. Or maybe I'm just a joker. Or a playboy. Whatever the reason, I've done a whole lot of living in my time, and I apologise for nothing. That's the punk in me. Actually, maybe that's what this is all about: me just trying to beat the system in the best way I know how.

But I'm no Summoner clone. I smoke and wear a trench coat but that is as far as it goes. You might, as a reader, say: does the world really need another paranormal investigator? Well, I would say, Ireland does. And Cork has always been a hot bed of the supernatural and the unreal. These days there is more money about, the church has lost its power and influence and there are different faces to be seen and languages to be heard on the streets. Everything has opened up. This means that the city is even more receptive to supernatural entities; ghosts and gods and everything in between. Its psychic 'other' life has become so much more interesting.

This does not automatically mean that there are more villains. Just like people, most entities are good. And bad things happen to good entities all the time. So, me and James, we're busier than ever. By the end of this narrative, if you think I'm just a lazy scrounger, that's okay. You're entitled to your opinion. If you think I'm just a dodger, that's fine too. A lot of people have called me fake over the years. It's the story of my life. Believe me. To those people I say the following. We all know that Cork is the 'real' capital. I've gotten to know this city well and the city has gotten to know me too. I can honestly look her in the eye, and she knows that I am real also. She's on my side. In fact, you could say we are dedicated to each other.

It might be a good idea to tell you my name, now. Steven Jones. That's me. They say names have power. If that's the case, I didn't get off to a very good start, did I? My partner's name is James McCarthy. As you probably know, that's a real Cork name. But it doesn't make him any more 'Cork' than I am. It's silly really: judging people by their names. Or their background. Or their faces. If you want to be Irish, if you want to be Corkonian, you only have to think and feel a certain way. You don't need anything else. That's a pretty radical way to think, even these days, but I'm a radical kind of guy. It comes with the line of work I'm in.

If you want to access the otherworld or the supernatural realm, call it what you want, you need to have a pretty extreme kind of mindset. In fact, it was that very question, about accessing the otherworld, that put everything in motion for us, one fateful day in Costigan's pub on Washington Street. But before I get to that, let me just talk briefly about our appearances. James is tall and melancholy, with soft, brown hair and a good-natured face.

Me? When I look in the mirror, I don't like what I see and I reckon most people don't either, so I've grown a beard to try to hide it. I have long, thinning blonde hair and a pair of slate blue eyes. As I said earlier, I wear a trench coat and I smoke a lot. Now, on to that day in Costigan's.

Costigan's was, and is, like many Cork pubs, lots of oakwood and framed posters and bygone era adverts on its walls. It's quite small. When we used to visit it, there weren't many students, which is surprising as it was the second closest pub to the University, next to The Thirsty Scholar. I don't know what a scholar's thirst is like, but it must be powerful judging by the way James used to drink. But, nevertheless, Costigan's was never a student pub. It has two levels: the upper level, which contains the bar and some tables and stools that run along-side it, and a lower one, which contains tables and benches, and at the end of which is a rear exit/entrance to the pub. As most of the clientele hung around the bar, the lower level afforded some privacy, especially in the afternoons, which is why me and James always drank there. It was also much quieter and laidback than the Thirsty.

So, there we were, one winter afternoon, drinking stout at our accustomed place in the lower level of Costigan's bar. We were halfway through our third pints. Me and James always drank more or less in sync with each other. We were on the same wavelength about a lot of things, as you might imagine, and we liked to keep it that way when drinking. It led to some very interesting conversations. So, as you probably know, when you are halfway through your third pint, you are in a kind of alcoholic twilight zone: you are not drunk yet but you know that you won't be leaving the bar for some time yet. And it is at this stage that some of the best conversations happen.

'So, how is college?' I asked him.

He picked up his pint glass and studied it for a few seconds before answering: 'It's exactly as I knew it would be: lecture halls, podiums, students, that sort of thing. Oh, and a goddamned big library.'

'You don't sound too impressed,' I said.

'Yeah, well, I was hoping to get invited to lots of parties and be even just a little bit popular, but it hasn't happened. It's like there's a barrier between me and the others. I don't know what it is but sometimes I feel so damned lonely and isolated.'

'You've only been there a couple of months. Maybe things will open up for you in time? Maybe it's like that for most of you...what do you call em?'

'Freshmen?'

'Yeah. Maybe you're not as alone as you think.'

'No. I don't think so, Steve. I look around and I listen, and it doesn't seem that way. Sometimes, it's like...' He sighed before continuing. 'It's like they are speaking a language that I can't speak. I can understand it, but I can't speak it. Does that make sense?'

'No,' I said, and we both laughed.

'Sorry if I've plunged the conversation into the depths,' he said.

'That's OK, man. Maybe there's someone you can see about this? A counsellor? A therapist?'

'You think I'm going mad?'

'No. Well maybe. Just a bit.'

'Thanks for the vote of confidence,' he said before lifting his glass and sinking the rest of his pint. When he had finished, he once more studied his pint glass and said, 'Language is such a powerful thing, Steve.'

'That's right,' I said.

'It can call up all sorts of things: angels, demons...'

'Now you're talking.'

There was a silence between us. James seemed to sigh and then lighten up in the same moment. 'Are you still thinking about becoming a magician?' he said.

'Yes. Beats getting a regular job, I reckon. I'm going to stay on the dole for a couple of years while I try it. That's the plan.'

'And how do you plan on going about it?'

'Well, I was thinking maybe you could help me with that, James. The truth is I don't know where to start.'

'Me? I know nothing about it.'

'Yes, but you're the one with the brain. You're the one with the logic. I just need to know where to start.'

James frowned and looked calmly over my shoulder into the middle distance before saying, 'I guess that it's a language. Just like the language of my fellow students. It's a language you have to learn. And like all languages, once you learn it, it will give you access to a whole new world.'

'See? Like I said. The brain. So, how do I learn it?'

'Books?' James said. 'Books of magic?'

'Is there any other way?'

'I suppose you could just invent your own language. Like William Blake did,' James said.

'Yes! I like the sound of that. Who's William Blake?' I said.

'Well, he was a great poet and mystic. He had visions. Visions of angels and demons. And he believed they were as real as you and me are. But at the same time, he believed that all deities reside in the human breast. He invented his own mythology. He was also very concerned with the plight of the working classes.'

'Sounds like my kind of guy. What do you mean by he invented his own mythology?'

'Well, he put down in his poetry his own mythology. Kind of like what Tolkien did. You know, when I think about it, isn't it something we all do? Self-mythologising? To help us make sense of our lives?'

'Yes,' I said. 'But what about the angels and demons? How did he access that world? That's what I want to know.'

'I don't know,' James said. 'His most famous quote is "The road of excess leads to the palace of wisdom". Maybe he was talking about magic?'

'The road of excess. Does that mean we have to take lots of drugs?'

'Hmmm...maybe. But there are other kinds of excess.'

'Yes, but not nearly as enjoyable, I bet,' I said and finished off my pint. 'My round.'

So, I got up and went to get two more pints. There were two guys propping up the bar in silence. I stood and waited: a tall, slender, intense young man in a trench coat. One of the barflies turned around just enough to look me up and down, then returned to the newspaper he was reading. Standing there, I had an intimation that I had a very long and hard journey ahead of me. And I was right.

I returned with the two pints.

'So, where were we?' I said.

'William Blake and excess.'

'Ah, yes. Does he have any other cool quotes like that?'

'I must create my own system or be enslaved by another man's. I'm paraphrasing.'

'I'm really getting to like this Blake guy. But we are still left with the question of how do we access the supernatural.'

'We? Am I part of your plans too?'

'Yes, of course. I need you as the brains of the operation. The 'book' guy.'

'Oh, you mean like Giles? In *Buffy the Vampire Slayer*?'

'Yes. Exactly.'

'Ok, so say we do manage to access the astral plane. And we learn a lot about magic. What do you plan on doing? I mean, what's the point?'

The point is to do some good. Just like John Summoner. Simple as that.'

'I don't know if John Summoner is such a good model, Steve.'

'I don't know of any other, do you?'

'What about Buffy?' James said and smiled.

'Ha bleedin' ha,' I said and gave him the finger. 'So, are you with me on this?'

'I don't know. Just what are you proposing?'

'A partnership. We work together for the good of the city.'

'I don't know. I'll help you out with accessing the supernatural but beyond that...'

'You will? That's great. What will you do?'

'I'll ask a Philosophy professor about it. I'll do it tomorrow. How's that?'

'Great. Thanks, James. You're a pal,' I said.

He looked over my shoulder again into the middle distance before returning his focus and asking, 'How is the band going?'

'Ok, I guess. We play a gig on Thursday night in Nancy Spains. You coming?'

'I'll try to make it. I've a lot of reading to do.'

'You need to get out more, man. I mean, I'm all for books, don't get me wrong, but I think you can do too much reading.'

'Aye. I'll try to make it. You guys are good.'

'And we're getting better. Or at least I am.'

'Hey. Maybe you could access the supernatural through music.'

I paused for thought. 'Interesting idea. How?'

'I don't know. There must be a way of interweaving the two. Music and magic.'

'Yes. There is. I think you're right. It's called Shamanism.'

'There you go.'

'James, you are a genius.'

'Don't mention it.'

'Could I look it up in the library? You know, in college?'

'I don't think so, Steve. You need to be a student to access it.'

'I am a student. A student of magic. As of now,' I said.

'Do you have an ID?'

I sighed and shook my head.

'Ok. I'll look it up for you.'

'No, James. You are doing enough for me as is. I'll look it up in the city library. Maybe we could meet up over a coffee, though?'

'You mean meet up in College?'

'Yes. After you talk to your professor friend.'

'Why not?'

'Cool. And maybe we could talk to some students and get you invited to a party.'

'Some things are beyond even magic, dude. So, I'll talk to my professor friend, and you look up Shamanism and we'll try to come up with some answers.'

'Yes! Ah, James. I think we are onto something here. It just feels right. The city needs us.'

'Let's just see how we get on. I'm not making any promises.'

So, there we were. Two young men with heads full of ideas and no experience of the world. No stories to tell. But, reader, bear with me. The stories will come. Muse, just give me the mind to tell them clearly and gracefully.

That night, I came home drunk but not completely out of it. I went into the sitting room where my father rested in an armchair, watching TV, as he was accustomed to. He was a quiet man with soft, deep, almost delicate blue eyes. That night they had the look of someone who is far away, as they often did. I fell back into the other armchair with my trench coat still on. There was a black and white film on the TV. Something with Burt Lancaster in it, an actor for whom my father had much admiration. But it hadn't the power to distract him from whatever was playing in his mind.

'I've come to a decision. About my future,' I droned, slowly but without slurring. 'I've decided to become a magician.'

My father kept his eyes on the TV. Burt Lancaster was talking affectionately to a little bird that was perched on his finger.

When it appeared that he had nothing to say on the matter, I got out of the chair and left the room but, as I was going, he said in a subdued voice, 'Be careful, Steven.'

'I will,' I said.

That night I was visited by John Summoner and Jim Morrison of The Doors. By 'visited' I mean in a dream, but it was really too lucid and coherent to be a dream. And John Summoner said it wasn't a dream. I suppose you would call it a psychic episode. But surely it had the same purpose as a dream. Carl Jung believed that dreams spoke to us a lot about our place in society and this 'dream' certainly did that for me.

So, I was standing in the midst of a swamp. It was night-time and a slow, serpentine mist crawled about the place. I recognised it as the home of the Green Man, the hero of a comic book I was into at the time. I looked about the place and there was no-one to be seen. Instead of exploring, I just took out a cigarette, lit it, and stood there, smoking. I was surrounded by the chorus of a thousand insects. I could hear creatures stirring in nearby water, upsetting it. I was a little afraid.

Soon, I heard the voices of two men, approaching. They talked in a subdued way, which somehow comforted me. I turned my head in their direction and the first thing I saw was the red tips of their cigarettes. This also soothed me as they put me in mind of lamp lights.

So, they got closer. I soon recognised John Summoner from his trench coat and accent. Morrison was harder to identify. It was the *LA Woman* period Morrison – a great, bushy beard and a green, baggy coat that looked like it was bought in an Army and Navy store. No leathers. No cheekbones. But the same dark, doomed eyes. So, these two heroes of mine approached. When they reached me, they stood before me, looking me up and down.

'Steven, innit?' Summoner said.

'Yes.'

'Do you know who we are?'

'Yes. You're John Summoner and you're Jim Morrison.'

'That's right, mate.' Summoner drew long on his cigarette and then flicked it away into the mist shrouded darkness. 'A little birdy told me that you want to become a magician. Is that right?'

'Yes. I do.'

'You sure about that?'

'Yes. Completely.'

'Well, mate. I'd warn you against it, but I can see that you are set on it.'

'But you're my inspiration...,' I said.

'Don't blame me, mate. I'm just a fictional character. Jim 'ere is real, of course. But a lot of fiction has been written about him. So, you can't blame him either. For being a role model, that is. Anyway, I'm here to give you some advice. But before that, Jim wants to say a few words about Shamanism, which I believe you are interested in?'

'Yes. That's right.'

'Hey, Steve,' Morrison said. I noticed that it wasn't a cigarette he was smoking but a cigar.

'Hi, Jim.'

'Now, don't quote me on any of this. I'm no expert. It's just my own thoughts...based on what I've read and learned through experience.'

'Ok, Jim.'

There was a silence as Morrison organised his thoughts. Then he began. 'When you perform...especially as a singer, you need to...go to the edge. And the best way to do this is through improvisation.

Improvisation...frees up energies. Psychic energies...which allow the Shaman to perceive the spirit realm or the supernatural realm, whatever you want to call it...Spontaneity and freedom are the keys to access the unknown. Just like they are the keys to creativity and art. Freedom is the...first condition of magic.'

When it was evident that he was finished, I asked, 'What about trance? Trance induced visions. Isn't that a big part of it?'

'That's right. And it was a big part of the Doors concert experience too. Hypnotic trance is similar to sleep. Like sleep it...allows the unconscious to become conscious...inducing a visionary state, as you say. Again, it's about freedom. Delivering people from the ordinary, the banal...the limited ways in which they think and feel.'

'How much of it is about words?'

'Man, it's all about words. All of it.'

'And what about drugs?' I asked.

Morrison sighed before saying, 'Yes, that is part of many Shamanic traditions but...you really have to know what you are doing. Be careful, man, is what I'd say to you on that score.'

'Listen to Jim,' Summoner said. 'Proper intellectual, inne? You any questions for me, mate?'

'Yes. How much of it is real and how much of it is just in your head?'

'Good question. I suppose what it comes down to is what do you want to believe? It's a choice. Like Jim says, it's about freedom. You are free to choose. To be or not to be, as the man said.'

'Yes, but I want to know how real is it? If I choose to believe, how will I experience it? Will I see things as you see them?'

'That I can't answer, mate. As I said, I'm just a fictional character. But I will say this: the world would be a helluva lot less interesting place to live in without magic in it.'

'So, do I have to, like, read many books? To become a magician?'

'Not really. Just play it by ear. And, as Jim 'ere says, improvise. All the reading can be done by your buddy, James, right? You got any more questions?'

'What about good and evil? Are they real?'

'Oh yes, mate. You won't need to be a magician to figure that one out.'

I nodded, pensively. 'One more question. What's the story with Chas? What was the favour you did for him? You know, to keep him always in your debt.'

Summoner laughed briefly before saying, 'Read no. 84. It's all in there.' He took out a packet of cigarettes from his coat and pulled one free. 'That it?' he said before lighting up.

'I guess so,' I said.

He looked around at the swamp. 'Any sign of the big green fellow?' he said.

'You mean the Green Man? No, I've not seen him.'

'If you see him around, tell him I was asking after him, will you?'

'But this is just a dream. I'll wake up any minute now.'

'Oh, it isn't, mate. This is real. This is as real as it gets.'

'But that means...didn't you say it was a matter of faith? Magic, I mean?'

Summoner laughed again and drew on his cigarette. 'Yeah, I contradict myself a lot. If I didn't, I'd go insane.'

'But I'll wake up from this, won't I? I'm not trapped here, am I?'

'You'll wake up, mate. Don't you worry about that. Anyway, we'd best be on our way. Cheerio, mate, and good luck with it, yeah?'

'Yes, cheerio mate,' Morrison said and grinned at the seeming quaintness of the expression.

So, they walked away. As they did so, they seemed to resume a conversation. 'In a way, I'm glad *Waiting for the Sun* didn't make it to the album of the same name, as *Morrison Hotel* would be a lot less good without it.'

'Yeah, I really like that song too. It's definitely one of our most under-rated songs.'

'It's also probably your heaviest. That and *Five To One*.'

'You mean lyrically or musically?'

'Musically, but I do like the lyrics a lot. "This is the strangest life I've ever known". Very Doorsy...'

The following afternoon, I met up with James in the college cafeteria, as planned. I got there a bit early and found myself a nice, comfortable corner, where I could sip my coffee and smoke and wait for my friend. I was a little hungover. Back then, hangovers weren't really a problem. I thought about the 'dream' I had had the night before. I had been thinking about it all morning. I wasn't disturbed or phased by it. In fact, I was excited. If I had John Summoner on my side then I was ready and able to take my first steps toward becoming a magician. As I replayed the meeting over and over in my head, I couldn't help but feel a surge of confidence and joy. Although I knew it not then, it was the joy of someone who has received a calling.

The place was busy but not crowded. As I waited, I tuned into the conversations that were taking place around me. '...no, I'm serious. He sang *My Way*. At the podium. In front of everyone. He is just totally in love with Frank Sinatra...Takes about three years to do one. The record is two. I'm going to do mine on Modernism...George Harrison played bass for the Beatles, didn't he? I could have sworn he did...spent the whole day in the college bar, drinking. And he was like, totally lucid. He must have drank really, really slowly...'

It didn't take long for me to realise that I was being observed. There was a girl sitting at a nearby table, smoking and watching me. She had long, dark, centre parted hair and wore a Jimi Hendrix t-shirt. There were bracelets and bangles on her arms and wrists. I had seen that look before, mainly in pubs. It was a kind of female student gaze. Perceptive. Open-minded. Absorptive. In a couple of years, that look would most likely be gone as reality showed its teeth. Alas, youth is fleeting. But at that moment I wasn't thinking of that. All I was thinking of was talking to her about Jimi Hendrix and maybe buying her another coffee. Just as I was about to get up and approach her, James showed up. I silently cursed him but then immediately felt bad about it.

'How's tricks?' I said as he sat down opposite me.

'Ok, I guess.' He put his coffee down on the table and also his sack of books.

'How's the head?'

'Fine. How many pints did we have yesterday?'

'Seven or eight,' I said.

'You still want to become a magician?'

'Yes. Now more than ever. Let me tell you about the dream I had last night. Only it wasn't a dream. More like a psychic episode.' So, I told him. I recalled everything clearly and this was another reason to believe that it wasn't just a dream.

'Interesting,' James said.

'Do you believe me? That it was real? Like John Summoner said?'

'I believe you that it wasn't just a dream.'

'Ok, I'll settle for that,' I said.

James sipped his coffee and then opened his sack. He took out a small, hard-cover book and placed it on the table between us. 'So, I talked to the professor about it.'

'James, you are a legend,' I said. 'What did he say?'

'He said that he didn't know much about magic. He said maybe to look up a Madam Blavatsky and something called the Theosophical Society. He also mentioned a guy called Aleister Crowley. Then he said I might look up Eastern Mysticism too. Especially Tibetan Buddhism. He said that there were lots of rituals and spells and supernatural things associated with it. So, I went to the library to do some research. There's a whole section devoted to religious studies, so I decided to look up Tibetan Buddhism. I didn't really have the time to look up Blavatsky or Crowley. Anyway, I found this.' He picked up the book and handed it to me. *The Little Book of Buddhism* it said on the cover. Below it was the author's name: Damien Gould. There was no illustration or image on it, just a plain yellow-gold background. I thumbed through it.

'There's a form of Buddhism known as Tantra which involves magic and spells. Here. Read this,' James said and took the book from me. He found a page and handed it back to me, tapping a finger on an area of text. I read it: *the Tantras are written in a mysterious twilight language that can only be accessed by initiates via a guru who teaches the meaning of the language. As in the Western tradition, Tantra makes use of magic circles, spells and charms.*

I looked up at James and said, 'Sounds promising.'

'Read the next page. The part about sex,' James said and grinned. So, I did.

Desire can be used as a means to liberation. The passions are a powerful form of energy, especially sexual passion, which, if properly channelled, can be used to achieve spiritual development. 'Very promising,' I said.

'Here,' James said and took the book from me again. He thumbed to another page and handed the book back to me, tapping, once more, on an area of text. *Many supernatural elements are found in Buddhist art and literature. These elements become more exaggerated as the centuries pass. Gods and spirits are often depicted as forming a part of the audience at important episodes in the Buddha's life.*

James once more took the book from me, thumbed through it and handed it back. *Not all monks are philosophers and many believe that mystical experiences, achieved through meditation, are a surer path to liberation than the study of texts...the experiential aspect is of great importance as Buddhists believe that the religious life is essentially a path to self-transformation. Meditation generates altered states of consciousness that speed up spiritual development...It is believed that in the fourth level of trance or Jhana, the meditator can gain psychic powers such as clairvoyance, telepathy and the ability to recall previous lives. They can also gain psycho-kinetic powers such as the ability to fly, walk on water and create duplicate bodies...visionary and ecstatic techniques that allow the construction of alternate realities and the gaining of magical powers. The third exercise involves the development of techniques of spontaneity to gain freedom...A search for a technique that aimed at enlightenment through a liberated mode of action.*

I looked up at James. 'Jim Morrison said that freedom is the first condition of magic. He talked about freeing up psychic energies in order to perceive the supernatural,' I said.

'Yes, there seems to be a lot of talk about freedom in there,' James said. 'Maybe he was right.'

'This is all kind of scattered in my head, James. I wish I knew what to do. I mean it's exciting and all, but it's not very instructive.'

'You want to borrow this book? Maybe study it? You're a student of magic after all.'

'No, not now. I think I'm going to try the shamanistic approach.'

'What will you do?' James said.

'I'm going to try it at the gig tomorrow. I'm going to put myself and the audience into a trance and see what happens.'

'Did you look it up in the City Library?'

'No, I think I got enough info from Morrison. Besides, Summoner said to play it by ear.'

James nodded his head and sipped from his coffee. I looked over his shoulder and was glad to see the female student still smoking and watching me.

'Well, if it doesn't work out you can always try the Eastern way,' James said.

'Meditation?'

'Yes. Here,' he said and took the book from me. 'You might find this interesting.' He found a page and handed it back to me. 'Read the part about Zen Buddhism,' he said.

Zen holds that the study of texts and doctrines can be a hindrance to spiritual awakening. It relies on humour, spontaneity, poetry and unconventional behaviour to communicate the idea of enlightenment.

'There it is again. The idea of freedom,' I said. 'That must be the key to all this.'

'Mind-forged Manacles,' James murmured, looking into the middle distance.

'What's that?'

'It's from William Blake. The idea that we have to liberate our minds if we want to attain vision.'

I nodded and looked over his shoulder at the girl again. She was now absorbed in a book, her face tranquil.

'Ok, here's what we'll do.' I returned my attention to James. 'I'll try the Shamanism tomorrow night at the concert and if it doesn't work, I'll call over to you and try the meditation.' I smiled and said, 'Isn't this exciting? I mean, this could work, James. This could work.'

James nodded and returned the smile. He picked up the book and put it back in his sack.

'Thanks for finding the book, as well. I owe you one. In fact, I'm going to repay you right now,' I said and got up from my seat, my eye on the girl.

'What are you doing?'

'I'm going to get you invited to a party.'

I went over to her.

When I reached her table, she looked up from the book. She had intelligent, hazel green eyes and olive skin. She didn't look too impressed by me. This wasn't going to be easy, I reckoned.

'Hello,' I said. 'I was just wondering what book you were reading?'

She showed me the cover of the book. *The Scarlet Letter* it said.

'Ah, I haven't read that. Is it any good?'

'Yes, it is,' she said, a little frostily.

I couldn't understand her attitude, when earlier she had been looking at me, as if checking me out. But I soldiered on. 'Mind if I join you?'

She sighed and put the book down, nodding her head, as if this happened to her all the time and she was getting a little tired of it.

So, I sat down. I looked her in the eye and smiled. She didn't return it but maintained eye contact. Boy, she was hard to read.

'You a student?' I asked.

She nodded.

'So am I. I'm studying magic,' I said, hoping to get a smile out of her. She didn't but she did raise an eyebrow, which was promising.

'I'm a freshman. Are you a freshman or...er...fresh person?'

She smiled and shook her head slightly. 'Yes,' she said. I was getting somewhere. I remembered some advice my father had given me in one of his more communicative moments. Make them laugh. If you wanted to pull, just make them laugh. So, I went for it.

'I was visited by Jim Morrison last night in a dream and he told me about Shamanism. I sing in a band, see, and I want to try it out in a concert we're playing tomorrow night. I'm going to try to access the supernatural world. If that doesn't work, I'm going to try meditating. Apparently, you can gain magical powers if you get to the right level of trance.'

She looked at me fixedly for a moment, her eyebrows lowered a little, causing a slight frown. Then she broke out into laughter, shaking her head again. She had a quiet laugh, and it didn't last long but I was much relieved. I laughed too.

'I'm not really a student. At least not here,' I said. 'But everything else I said is true.'

She laughed some more before composing herself again. She returned to that female student gaze I mentioned earlier. Calm and quietly perceptive. I knew that she was probably way more intelligent than I was, but I didn't let this stop me. I wouldn't let a few brain cells get in the way of scoring with this lovely, enigmatic creature.

'What are you studying?'

'English, Philosophy, Sociology and Greek and Roman Civ.,' she listed.

'My friend back there is studying English, too.' I turned round in my chair and looked at James. He raised a hand in response. I turned back to her and said, 'He's having a bit of a difficult time. He's not been asked to go to any parties, see?'

'You mean he's lonely,' she said.

'Yes. The loneliness of crowds I guess you'd call it.'

'He's not alone.'

'That's what I said to him, but he has trouble believing it.'

I took out my packet of cigarettes and offered her one. She looked at them a bit hesitantly before taking one.

'Take two. I noticed you smoking earlier. I imagine you don't have much money, being a student and all.'

'One is enough, thanks,' she said. 'Do you work?'

'No, I'm on the dole. I going to try this magic gig for a while, see how far I get with it. If it doesn't work out, I'll get a proper job.'

'You serious?'

'Mmm,' I said, lighting my cigarette and then lighting hers. 'You don't believe in it?'

She shrugged. 'It sounds like fun but...I've never really encountered it.'

'Keep your mind open.' I leant back in my chair and looked at her and smiled. 'So, do you get invited to many parties?' I asked her.

'I've been to a couple.'

'Do you think you could bring my friend back there to one? All you have to do is bring him along. You don't have to hold his hand or anything.'

She sighed and said, 'I'll see what I can do.'

There was a moment of silence and I smiled at her in an arch kind of way.

'What about you?' she asked.

'What about me?'

'Do you like to party?'

'Yeah, if it's with the right people.'

'What does that mean? Don't you like students?'

'I like them fine. They're a bit annoying, present company excluded, but I don't have anything against them.'

She nodded, smoking, and thinking in that cool, perceptive way.

'What are you thinking?' I asked her.

'Never you mind,' she said, and smiled, expelling smoke from her mouth.

'I like your t-shirt.'

'Thanks.'

'Be careful with it. If you wash it too much, it will fade away.'

'And I, being a poor student, haven't got many clothes to spare. You shouldn't think in cliches.'

'You're right. I shouldn't. So, what are you loaded?'

'No, but that's not the point. Where are you from anyway?'

'I'm from Cork.'

'This *is* Cork,' she said.

'Yeah, I know, but sometimes when I come up here it feels like a different...place. A place outside of Cork.'

She raised her eyebrows, considering. 'It does have its own atmosphere.'

'Where are you from?'

'Tipperary.'

I smiled and nodded. 'I had you figured as a Tipperary woman, alright.'

'Is that right, Cork?'

'Yes,' I said.

She laughed again, blowing smoke out of her lips. I was really getting somewhere with her.

'I have to go to a lecture,' she said, picking up the book she had been reading and placing it inside her bag.

'So, will you help my friend out? About going to a party?'

She sighed and then pressed her lips together. She reached into her bag and pulled out a notepad with a pen stuck in its spine. She liberated the pen and wrote on a page. When she had finished, she pulled out the page and handed it to me, whilst crushing out her cigarette in the small tin ashtray.

I read what she had written. It was in no mystical language. It needed no study or interpretation. No guru to translate it. It was just a name and a number. But boy it made you feel good to be alive.

Miranda
296 487

I folded the piece of paper and put it in the breast pocket of my shirt. 'Ok, so I'll give you call, yeah?'

'Do,' she said, putting on her green leather jacket. When she had finished, she looked at me, as if she expected something. 'So?' she said.

'So what?'

'Aren't you going to give me your name?'

'Oh, right. Yeah, it's Steve. Steve Jones.'

'What's his name?' she said, indicating James with her head.

'His name is James.'

'So, you want to party?'

'Yes!'

'Both of you?'

'Sure!'

'Ring me. I'll see what I can do.'

She smiled one more time and then turned around and walked away. She walked slowly and a little self-consciously, with her head lowered. Somehow this made her even more attractive.

I returned to James, grinning and triumphant. 'I got her number, man.'

'She going to take you to a party?'

'She's going to take *us* to a party.'

'Yeah? Where and when?'

'I don't know, James. I don't know. But I got her number!' It was as if I'd won the lottery or something. I sat down opposite James again.

He leaned forward, his arms on the table. 'I've been thinking,' he said.

'You're always thinking, James. You think too much.'

'Yeah, I know. I've been thinking about your gig tomorrow. About you being a Shaman. I was thinking, maybe you could try reading from *Finnegans Wake* by James Joyce.'

'Finnegans what?'

'Finnegans Wake. It's a book that's written in a language he invented. It's almost impossible to read. See, I was thinking about this mysterious language that the Buddhist monks use in Tibet. This 'twilight' language. You know that I showed you in the book earlier? And it just popped into my head that *Finnegans Wake* might be considered as a Western version of that language. Also, it ties in with the Freedom theme. It is a language that's liberated from meaning.'

I looked at him, slightly awed. 'Wow. That's good thinking, James. But Morrison said I should improvise.'

'Maybe you could do that as well. Two minds are better than one. It would certainly make for an interesting gig.'

'It's a great idea James. You're an intellectual ball of fire, you know that? Where can I get a copy of this book?'

'Try Waterstones. It's underneath the library. I'll go with you,' James said.

As we walked through the cafeteria, towards the exit, I said to him, 'do you have *Shot To Hell* no. 84, by any chance?'

'You want to what?' Ian said. He stood there looking at me with an expression of mild exasperation on his face. He had a dark complexion. Everything about Ian was dark: his clothes, his hair, his eyes, and his humour. He could be a right moody bastard.

'I want to read from *Finnegans Wake*. It's a book by James Joyce,' I said.

We were hanging out in the small backstage area at Nancy Spain's Bar and Live Venue. We liked playing at Nancy Spain's and one of the reasons was this backstage area, which made us feel like we were the business. I was sitting on a large oaken table, my feet dangling, holding a bottle of beer. While Ian stood before me, frowning, his hands in the side pockets of his black leather jacket.

'Why?' he demanded.

Myself and Ian never really got on. There was friction there from the first time we jammed together as a band. I remember it well. Back then, the only band-rooms available to rent were these squalid little rooms located in a building on Paul's Street, which is now called Rory Gallagher Plaza. They were literally just rooms with a couple of sockets on the walls. And they were small. Real small. I don't know how we managed to get all the gear in there and still find room for ourselves. And don't ask me about the toilet.

It sounds depressing but the truth is I had a lot of good times in that band-room. Drinking two litre bottles of cider, smoking hash, and rapping away. Can't avoid the old platitude here: we were poorer, but we were happier.

Anyway, I won't go into the history of how we got together as a band. It was the same as any music scene: you got to know people and people who knew people. Word spread. It just happened.

When the band started, I was playing bass. I wasn't much good, which is part of the reason why I was transferred to vocal duties not long after. So, there we were. The four of us crowded into this shitty, graffitied little room, jamming for the first time. I know that the bass and drums are supposed to lock in with each other to form a good rhythm section. Part of me thinks that maybe that was why he said what he said. Because it was important for the band that we get on. But I think the real reason was because he was being an insensitive asshole. I was a very shy and awkward kid. I found it hard to make eye contact with people, never mind talk to them.

So, after we jammed a couple of songs, Ian says to me, 'Hey, why don't you look at me? Don't you like me? Have you something against me?' I was a bit mortified and had absolutely no idea what to say. 'Why don't you like me? Is it something I said?' he pressed the issue.

The other two went silent. I never answered him. Not because I was pissed at him, which I should have been, but because I just didn't know what to say. So, that's the kind of guy Ian was. I don't bear him any ill will. It wasn't always like that between us. We shared some jokes and good times. He once paid me the considerable compliment of being 'wasted as a front man.' I also got him into *The Sandman*, another comic book I was, and still am, enamoured with.

'I just want to try something different,' I lied. 'Don't you think it would be cool?'

'No, I don't Steve,' he said. 'Rock music and poetry don't mix.'

'Yes, they do! What about the Doors? Or My Dying Bride? Or Mad Season?'

'Let me see it.'

So, I picked up the book that was lying beside me and handed it to him. I braced myself for his reaction. I knew this was going to take some convincing.

He opened the first page and read for maybe half a minute. 'What is this gibberish?' he said, looking up at me. 'I mean, what is it?'

I have a strange sense of humour and often find myself laughing alone. It has gotten me into some trouble over the years. Moments when I tried but failed to resist. This was one of those moments. I started to laugh. I have a quiet laugh but when I start it lasts for a long time. Billy, our guitarist, says it's because I have a good imagination. I think there might be some truth in that.

'What are you laughing at Steve?' Ian said in his most exasperated tones.

'Sorry,' I said. I lowered my head in humility, but my frame still shook with the laughter.

The other two came in. They were in good spirits, each holding a pint of stout, and their lively conversation spilled into the room.

'What's the joke?' Amber, our bass player, said. She was very tall and laidback and intelligent. She wore a frilly white shirt and a pair of corduroy green trousers.

'This clown wants to recite this during the gig,' Ian said and handed the book to her.

She looked at the cover. 'Ah, the Wake,' she said. I continued to shake with laughter.

'Let me see,' Billy said, grinning sympathetically.

Me and Billy got on very well. He was a few years older than me, and he often critiqued and advised me about my behaviour both on and off stage but, for the most part, we were on the same wavelength. He was a good-looking guy: tall with long, tawny hair that reached past his shoulders. Like Amber, he was incredibly intelligent, but he had a humility and earthiness which offset it. Plus, he drank like a fish. He was a fun guy to be around. That night he wore a blue plaid shirt and white denims that were torn at the knees.

He looked in the book and read a few lines before breaking into laughter himself.

'Ah come on. Don't you start,' Ian said.

Billy handed the book back to Amber, who opened a random page and began to read. As she did so, a small frown of concentration appeared on her brow.

'He thinks it would be cool to read from it,' Ian said.

'Why not? I think it's a great idea,' Billy said. He looked at me and laughed some more. But I was coming to the end of my fit.

'It's not just because I think it would be cool. It's an experiment. I want to try to put myself and the audience into a shamanic trance.'

'A shamanic trance?' Ian said and shook his head.

'Are you serious?' Amber said.

'Yes, I am. I want to try it near the end of the gig. If it doesn't work, we can just say we were mixing poetry and music.'

'What do you plan on doing?' Amber said, looking at me steadily. She was a proper bass player. Cool, sensible, reliable. The backbone of the band.

'I'm not really sure. Just read from the book and play it by ear, I guess. But I need you guys to provide a steady, constant hypnotic riff.'

Amber handed the book back to me and said, 'I'm up for it.' She smiled, drank from her pint and belched. A solid belch. A bass player's belch.

'Me too,' Billy said.

'Ok. Majority rules. But don't blame me when we end up the laughing stock of the Cork music scene. Nobody's going to get this,' Ian said.

'I only want to try it this once,' I said.

'We'll never live it down,' Ian insisted. 'You could at least have gotten something intelligible. Not this gibberish.'

'It's a twilight language. The idea is to put myself in to a state of…somewhere in between wakefulness and sleep. To give me access to the spiritual realm.'

'Do you even know what you are doing? You sound totally unprepared,' Ian said.

'Like I said. I'm going to play it by ear.'

Ian shook his head in resignation. 'I'll go along with this. But remember, I warned you.'

'Thanks guys,' I said. Amber smiled and nodded. Billy grinned and gave me the thumbs up. I didn't look at Ian. Couldn't bring myself to. Couldn't face the scowl that I knew was on his face.

Nothing happened.

We came to the last song in our set and added a coda. A slow and steady droning riff that lasted a few minutes. I opened *Finnegans Wake*, picked a random page, and began to read. And nothing happened. Ian's prediction of becoming a laughing stock did not materialise. The crowd actually seemed to enjoy it, judging by their enthusiastic applause at the end of it.

'That's a bit of Finnegans Wake for ye,' I said and winked and saluted the crowd before leaving the stage.

Back stage, the others didn't seem disappointed or cross. Even Ian looked placid. It had been a good gig. The reading hadn't spoiled it. In fact, the marriage of poetry and rock had gone quite well. I felt a profound sense of relief, which kind of surprised me. I had had little awareness of just how much was riding on my shamanic experiment when I walked out on stage. The others had put their faith in me, and I knew, whatever happened, my place in the band wouldn't be any less secure, but if the experiment had turned out to be a stinker it could have really hurt us. It could have tarnished the name of the band. So, when I returned to the oaken table and sat on it with a fresh bottle of beer in my hand and my feet dangling, I was not a disappointed man.

But nothing had happened. Why? Well, the answer was simple, really. I should have tried improvising. Wasn't that what Morrison had said to me? To free up psychic energies you need to go to the edge and improvise? Freedom was the first condition of magic? Yes, that was the reason. So why didn't I try it? Well, the truth was I was too afraid. Wouldn't anyone be? The chances of screwing it up and falling over the edge were too great. Yes, I was too afraid. Too afraid of falling. Too afraid of falling and dying. I wasn't a disappointed man, but I did let just a hint of regret into my after-gig beer buzz.

You'd expect that this hint of chagrin would be drowned out after a few bottles of beer. Not so with me. As I drank, the seed of regret grew until it was a like a bruised apple, sitting there, waiting to be tasted. I couldn't resist. You see you have to understand what kind of a drunk I am. I am an arrogant drunk. I think and feel that I'm invincible when I'm after several pints. Of course, it all goes downhill very soon after this but for an hour or so I am superman, immune to the effects of excessive alcohol consumption. So, I was just getting to this phase, and I couldn't let the apple alone. How could I have failed? I had John Summoner and Jim Morrison as friends, for Christ's sake. I was well connected. I was a serious person. Now, if things had taken their natural course, I would have got shit faced and woke up with little memory of the night before. As I said earlier, hangovers were not a problem for me at that age, but I was not immune to making an ass of myself and remembering only fragments of it the next morning. But things did not take their natural course. Not that night.

So, my superman phase was just peaking when I decided to leave the party and check in on James. We had agreed that, if the attempt at Shamanism had failed, we would try the Eastern way. I looked at my watch: it was approaching midnight. It was about a ten-minute walk to his bedsit. He would most likely still be up. Enjoying the company of a good book. So, I said my goodbyes. Billy and Amber were sad to see me go. I was just about to leave the backstage area when I felt a hand on my shoulder. I turned around and there was Ian. He had an intense look in his dark eyes. 'I'm sorry, Steve,' he said.

'It's ok, man,' I said. 'I don't blame you. It was a risky thing to do.'

'You heading off?'

'Yes. I'm going to a friend of mine's gaff. Going to try meditating. You know, to access the astral plane.'

Ian laughed. 'You're a crazy man,' he said.

'I know. Don't tell anyone.'

'Take care, Steve.'

When I left Nancy Spain's, the fresh air revivified my system. I strode up Barrack Street, the back of my trench coat sustained in the air behind me, like a cape. I didn't see a soul. I was somewhat sobered but there was still enough alcohol in my body to give me an enhanced feeling of power. Even though I had failed at my attempt at Shamanism, I knew that the night was not yet done with me. I had a date. A date with destiny. Did Buddhists believe in destiny, I wondered? James would know. James knew just about everything. He was the brain. I was the balls. I was struck by the aptness of this metaphor and smiled.

Yes, I was the balls. The action man. The dancer. Don't get me wrong. I was a book lover too. It's just that I had a role to play. Society demands that we take a role. And my role was to be a magician. To look after the psychic life of the city. To protect and serve, as they say. Yes, I would be the action man. I would be at the front. But I still had no idea of what I was facing.

So, I reached the apartment complex where James was living. I pushed the button for his bedsit and waited for him to come down and let me in. I waited a half a minute before pushing the button again. After another half a minute, the door was opened. There was a young man with a crazed expression on his face. He was ghost pale and his eyes were wide. He was wearing a pair of track-suit pants and his upper body was naked. He looked at me, crazed and panting.

'James? Is that you?' I asked.

'Steve! O, Steve! Thank God it's you. Thank God it's you!'

He grabbed my shoulders and then drew me into the hallway before shutting the door.

'What happened, James?'

He didn't answer. Just ran up the stairs without looking back. So, I followed.

When he came to the front door of his bedsit, he tried putting the key into the lock but his hands were shaking so badly that he couldn't do it.

'Would you?' he said and held out the small bunch of keys for me to open the door. So, I did.

Inside, the first thing I noticed was piles of books, arranged in a circle on the floor. James sat on the edge of his bed. He looked like he was struggling to catch his breath.

'What happened, man?' I said.

He looked at me, still panting. He was silent for a few seconds before saying, 'do you see them?'

'See who?'

He shook his head, looking distressed.

'See who, James?' I insisted.

'How did the gig go?'

'I tried it. It didn't work.'

He nodded. 'I thought that. I thought that.'

'James, what the Hell is going on?'

'I tried it,' he said.

'Tried what?'

'To access the supernatural. Through meditating. Jesus, Steve, you wouldn't believe what I'm seeing here.'

'What did you do?'

'I made a circle with those books,' he said, indicating the piles on the floor. 'That's why it didn't work for you, Steve. You need a circle. It's simple really. I just thought about those Fairy rings. You know. With the stones planted in a circle? I…I guessed that it's a way to separate the sacred and the profane. A boundary. And I…it's also a way of containing the magic. Simple really. Should have thought of it sooner.' He looked down at his hands, which were still shaking. But his breathing was becoming more regular.

'Go on,' I said. It was as much to talk him down as it was to find out what had happened.

'So, I made a circle with those books. And I prepared to meditate. I needed something to contemplate. I remembered what I said to you about *Finnegans Wake*. So, I tried it. I opened the book and picked a sentence. Something to meditate on. A mantra, they call it. I picked a sentence…'

'What did you pick? Do you remember?'

'Course I do. I meditated on it for over half an hour. "Television kills telephony in brother's broil." I sat inside the circle, with legs crossed and I did it. I just started meditating. It was hard at first but I…I got good at it. I did it for about thirty minutes. And I did feel tranced out a bit. But when I recalled myself and looked around the room, there was nothing out of the ordinary. I didn't feel any different. All I felt was a bit sleepy. So, I went to bed and fell asleep. And when I woke up…Jesus, Steve. My heart was thumping like mad. I thought I was going to die. And when I closed my eyes…Jesus Christ, Steve!'

'What was it? What did you see?' I said.

James put his head in his hands and shook it slowly. 'I saw…I…I think I saw God, Steve.'

'God? You think you saw God?'

'It was a mandala. And it was so bright and beautiful but above all…so perfect. So perfect, Steve. And I could see it so clearly. It was like a photograph. In my mind. Then I opened my eyes, and I could see them. Everywhere. Spirits. Ghosts. But also more tangible creatures. Fairies I suppose you would call them. Fairies and goblins and…well, things I have no name for.'

James' breathing had returned to normal and the freaked out look on his face was replaced by something approaching sanity.

'Can you still see them?'

'Yes.'

I have to admit I felt just a small pang of envy. James had succeeded where I had failed, and he had done it through intelligence and talent.

'Jesus, Steve. I'm just afraid that it will always be like this.'

'I don't think it will.'

He raised his head from his hands and looked at me. His eyes had definitely lost the crazed look they had had when he opened the door to me.

'Feeling better?' I asked.

'Yes. Much.'

If I hadn't been much of a friend, I would have left him then. But I didn't. I continued to talk to him. Keeping him down. Making sure he was going to be ok. I guess I'm not such a bad guy after all. Or at least I wasn't back then.

'Is there anything else you did? Anything that you might have forgotten?' I said.

'No. Don't think so. Why do you ask?'

'Because I want to try it. Remember, it was me who wanted it. I was going to try this if the Shamanism didn't work.'

'You mean you want this? How could you want this?'

I sighed and said, 'James, you are a very intelligent man. A man of reason. Intellect. Enlightenment. Me? I'm more of an imaginative type. A dark ages kind of guy. What freaked you out might not have the same effect on me. Do you understand?'

'But it seems so real,' he said.

'Yes. You've accessed another plane of existence. But I don't think you'll be stuck in this trip forever. I don' t think it works that way. This is maybe a kind of initiation?'

'So, there is no way back?'

'I don't know James. You're the one with the brains. I'm the balls.'

'The balls? What the hell does that mean?'

I smiled and shook my head. 'It's just something I thought up. Look James, whatever happens, one thing is clear. We are a team now. Whether you like it or not.'

'Don't I get a say in this?'

'You already made up your mind. When you chose to make that circle and sit in it and try it. Why else would you do it?'

'I guess you're right.'

'You know I am,' I said.

'So, when are you planning on doing it?'

'Tonight. When I get home.' James nodded pensively and there was a silence before I asked, 'You want me to stick around for a while?'

He nodded. 'Just a while. If you don't mind too much?'

'Ok. I don't mind at all, my friend.'

I got home at about 4am, having walked all the way. Back then, taxis weren't so readily available. It was a quiet, starry night. There was a hint of a sweet smell in the air. Like a sweet factory was nearby. There wasn't a soul.

When I arrived home, I was too exhausted to do anything but sleep. So, I went upstairs to my bedroom and collapsed on my bed with my trench coat still on. Within a few minutes I was gone.

I had another dream or psychic episode or
call it what you will.

I was standing by the sea. It was daytime
and the weather was rough. Stormy. Waves
boomed and crashed on the shore and the
water hissed as it was drawn back, as if in
protest. My trench coat snapped about me in
the wind. A reproving kind of snap. My face
was wet, and my eyes were squinting from the
spray. I looked around me. There was a man
about a hundred metres away down the beach.
He was dressed in a white suit and had a black
bowler hat on his head. He appeared to be
dancing. A kind of parody of Irish dancing.
His legs were flying about, backwards, and
forwards and sidewards and every which way.
He held out a walking stick, brandishing it as
if he were fencing with the wind.

'Hey, Steve,' I heard a voice say. I turned
around and there was Jim Morrison, once
more clad in his green army and navy coat.
His hands were buried deep in its side
pockets, and he was grimacing against the
wind and spray.

'Hello, Jim,' I said. 'Fancy meeting you
again.'

He managed a smile and nodded but didn't
say anything. He just looked out at the sea.

'You were right. I should have improvised.
Instead of reading from that book,' I said.

Morrison nodded and said, 'Maybe. I like
what your friend said, though. About it being
a language liberated from meaning?'

'You're obsessed with freedom, aren't you, Jim?'

'Yeah, I guess so.'

'What's it like being dead?'

'I don't want to spoil it for you, Steve.'

I looked out at the sea again. It suddenly struck me how monstrous it was.

'Does it make you feel small?' Morrison said, as if he could read my mind.

'Yeah, it does.' I looked down at the dancing man again. 'Who's that?'

'That, my friend, is Mr. James Joyce. Doing his famous spider dance.'

'Ah. I hope he isn't upset about us using his book.'

'I don't think he would be. You can go and ask him if you want.'

'No. He looks…preoccupied.' Nothing was said and the elements lashed us for a while. 'So, I'm going to try meditating. To access the unknown,' I said, at last. 'Do you think it will work?'

'I don't know, Steve. I don't know much about it. I'm an Occidental man.'

'It worked for my buddy, James.'

'Yes, it did. But what worked for him, might not work for you.'

'So, what are you saying? I might never be a magician?'

'Nothing in life is set in stone, Steve.'

'I thought you were on my side! You and Summoner! Where is he by the way?'

'Preoccupied. And I am on your side. Wouldn't be here if I wasn't.'

'So, tell me what to do, Jim. What do I do?'

'I think you need a good long sleep.'

'That's it? This is hopeless. I'll never become a magician.'

'One thing I learned in life is that if you want something badly enough, it will probably never happen.'

I sighed and said, 'Thanks Jim. Thanks for nothing.'

'I like storms,' Morrison said, looking out to sea again. 'Do you like storms, Steve?'

'Not particularly.'

'I get a powerful feeling when I'm amidst a storm. Just me and the elements. The storm is powerful but not as much as I am. Do you understand?'

'No,' I said, despondently.

'I've learned something, Steve. I've learned that power comes from inside. It's not something that can be given or conferred on you. It's not something that can be gained from a book. Not real power. You've got so much power inside you, Steve. If you don't become a magician, you're going to do *something*. That's for sure.'

'Sorry, if I don't seem enthusiastic, Jim. I'm a bit crestfallen here.'

'That's ok, man. Anyway, I must leave you.' Morrison said and patted me on the shoulder.

'That's it? That's all you have to say?'

'What do you want me to say, Steve?'

'I don't know. Will I see you again?'

'Maybe. Like I said, nothing is set in stone.'

'Except death,' I added, morosely.

'No, not even death. If I was dead, would I be here with you, having this conversation? No. It goes on, Steve. It goes on. Now, go back to sleep.'

'One more question, Jim. Summoner said you were a Shaman. Have you ever seen a ghost?'

'Can't say I have. Not a real ghost.'

'So, why are you here?'

'Hmmm. Maybe it's because I'm someone you know and don't know. Like the author of a book. Does that make sense?'

'No, it doesn't. But I'll have a think about it.'

'You do that,' he said and smiled and winked. 'Cheerio, Steve.'

Then he began to walk away.

'Jim!' I called to him. He turned around. 'It's sláinte! In Ireland we say sláinte!'

'Sláinte, Steve!'

Then he walked away in the direction of James Joyce, who was still dancing his spider dance. When he reached him, he put a hand on Joyce's shoulder, and he stopped dancing. Jim spoke something into his ear and then the two of them walked away down shore. Jim kept his hand on Joyce's shoulder and continued to talk into his ear.

I looked out at the monstrous sea. I didn't feel powerful at all. Just very, very small. I checked my coat for a packet of cigarettes. There was none.

Where was John Summoner when you needed him?

When I woke up the next morning, I felt strange. Even before I opened my eyes. I was lying on my back, which was unusual for me. I prefer to sleep on my side. And there was a powerful scent in my nose. A kind of earthy, flowery smell. I could hear the sound of breathing. It was very close. A kind of excited breathing.

I opened my eyes and there was a woman's face a few inches from my own. Her skin was green, and her eyes were a pale gold. Her hair was also green. But it wasn't human hair. It looked like leaves of grass, grown to a length of a few inches. She was grinning at me. 'What...?' I said.

She shushed me, putting a finger to her lips. Then she sat up. She was astride me, her body naked and as green as her face. Her breasts were pert. Her ribs showed a little but in a sexy way.

'Good morning, handsome,' she said.

'Who - ?'

'Ah, ah, ah,' she said. 'Listen to me now. My name is Sing. I'm here to welcome you to the other side.'

'You mean - ?'

'Shhhhhh. No talking. Just listening. So, you've woken up. You've made it to the astral plane. Well done! Now, you must decide what you are going to do. Are you going to work for the good of the city? Are you going to be on the front-line? Fighting the good fight, as they say? Just nod if that's a yes.'

I nodded.

'Good. Very good. That means you'll be seeing a lot more of me in the future. But you must understand, there is no going back. Once you're in, you're in. Same for your friend, James. He's a good lad to have on your side, by the way. That was good thinking about the circles. What else do I have to say? O, yes. It's not going to be easy. You've chosen the road less travelled, as the poet said. But you will be rewarded. As long as you stay on our side. Understood?'

I nodded again.

'Good. We are going to get along just fine. Remember, if you ever find yourself in a pickle, just play it by ear. Just like I do,' she said and raised her head and looked at the ceiling and began to sing:

We're gonna be just fine. You and I. You and I.

If you just sing, everything will be alright.

The city needs you. My magic boy. My magic boy.

Her voice was high but not piercing. Her pitch was flawless.

Then she laughed. She had a bubbly, frothy kind of laugh. She looked down at me again. 'You've got to be able to laugh, Stevie. You're not going to get very far if you can't laugh.'

So, I forced a laugh. I felt strange and a little afraid.

'Don't be afraid. It's a terrible thing to live life in fear. Just laugh and play it by ear,' she said and cocked her head slightly, looking pleased with the rhyme she had made. 'Now, seen as you've been such a good boy, I'll allow you one question. Just one. So, choose carefully.'

'Will I be seeing John again? John Summoner?'

She sighed and said, 'Yes. You'll be seeing him again. Him and his trench coat and his...God, he thinks he's so cool! Anyway, I must be off. Take care Stevie and we'll see you again, soon. Bye!'

Then she was gone. I sat up just in time to see her green bum disappear around the door to my room, leaving it ajar slightly. She left a sweet, earthy fragrance that lasted for days, reminding me that it hadn't been just another dream or psychic episode.

So, that's the story of how I got started. That's how I got into this game. Make of it what you will. You might still think I'm a fake. A charlatan. An imposter. But there is nothing I can do about that. All I can say is I've given my life to this city. I've taken the blows. I've gone to the edge. I've gone over the edge. I've given the very blood in my veins. All for this city. If you can believe this, read on. If not, close the book and walk away. Because if you don't believe me now, you never will.

II

You're probably wondering about Miranda.

I called her a few days after my awakening, and we got together pretty fast. We had good chemistry. Or maybe in our case you would call it alchemy. I told her about myself and James, our plans, and intentions, and she wanted in on it too. So, I had to find a way in for her. We tried meditation but it didn't work. It was clear that I would have to find another way. So, I asked John Summoner.

Where did I find him? Well, I didn't really. He came to me, again, as I was dreaming. He said he could get Miranda 'inside' but it would cost me. I'd have to return the favour some time. I'd be in his debt. I wondered if that debt would ever be fully repaid but I agreed as I didn't want to let Miranda down. He told me to bring her to a pub called the Grove, which was on Lavitt's Quay. He said there was a beer garden there that was a Liminal: a place where the natural and supernatural converge. So, we met up. Summoner had a pint of cider and a few cigarettes, and we talked for a while about what was happening in *Shot To Hell* and what to expect. Miranda remained silent. She later told me that she didn't like him. That he left her cold. And she still doesn't like him to this day.

After he had finished his pint, he got down to business. He said he was going to hypnotise

Miranda and cast a few spells while she was under. She looked uncomfortable with this but told him to go ahead. So, he picked up his zippo lighter, sparked up a flame and hypnotised her with it. Then he made some incantations. They were in Latin and sounded impressive. He dropped his Cockney accent for a steady intonation. When he was finished, he closed his zippo with a clap and snapped his fingers.

'That's you done,' he said. Then he got up and said, 'I'll be seeing you around, yeah?' He winked and was gone.

So, did she get us invited to any parties? Well, she didn't have to, really. She'd go and we'd just tag along. That's how it is with students. A bit risky but it definitely makes things more interesting and unpredictable. And by a strange coincidence, it was through Miranda's student friends and acquaintances that we got our first case. Turns out there was this ghost who was haunting their parties. This poor harmless fecker would suddenly appear, usually in an empty chair, and just sit there and freak everybody out. It had happened at three different houses when Miranda told us about it.

So, we went to our first student party and our first job at the same time. The ghost shows up and everyone bolts it. I can hear the sound of girls sobbing and guys cursing on the street outside. At first, I felt like running myself, but I forced myself not to. I was the balls of the operation, wasn't I? And this was the business

I wanted to go into. I'd likely have to face much worse than this in the future. I turned around looking for James but there was no sign of him. So, I looked at the ghost and he looked at me with a sort of sheepish, apologetic expression on his face. I pulled up a chair and sat opposite him and we talked.

Turns out he was just like James: a student who had never gotten invited to any parties. He had died in a traffic accident while he was a freshman. He said he didn't want to move on until he had been to a few parties. I told him he couldn't keep turning up, scaring the bejesus out of everyone. He said he knew that, but he didn't know if there'd be any parties in the afterlife. So, he was reluctant to go.

After some thought, I asked him had he ever read the Asterix comic books? He said he had. I reminded him of the great feast the Gauls had at the end of every book, after Asterix had done his work. It would be out in the open and there would be lots of mead and fresh cooked meat and everyone would be singing and laughing and in high spirits. And even though it happened at the end of every book, it always made you feel good. Why? Because it appeals to our spirit. I said that I believed the afterlife would be something like that. This seemed to satisfy him. He smiled and thanked me and disappeared and was never seen again.

I should clarify something here. There's been a lot of talk about accessing the supernatural or the astral plane or whatever you want to call it. So, how did these students see this ghost? Did they have access to it as well? The answer is no. They saw it for the same reason all regular people see ghosts. Because they have 'crossed over' to our world. Usually, it is because of unfinished business. Things that need resolving. And very often all that is required is a conversation. I've talked with so many ghosts over the years. Trying to understand their needs and issues. Trying to resolve them. A lot of the time it works. But not all ghosts are good. You can get some nasty ones too. Ghosts that there is no talking to. Some of them won't even look at you. So, you have to find other ways of getting rid of these.

So, I've been sitting here thinking about what to tell you. I have so many tales about our exploits over the years. But, as I said earlier, does the world really need another paranormal investigator? I think what the world needs is stories. That's all it has ever needed. And there are those I know who are far better story tellers than I am. So, I've decided to record some of their stories here for you. Yes, I've decided to tell you about the great epic pub crawl of the summer of 1999.

By then, Miranda and James had finished college. She had a living making and selling Gothic jewellery. She was pretty good at it too. She had a stall in the English Market. Mostly she made necklaces with pendants. Skulls, bats, gargoyles. That sort of thing. But

she also made pendants that you wouldn't call
Gothic. African tribal masks. Roman coins.
Celtic knots. I've even used her jewellery in
my work. Sometimes talismans are needed to
confront hostile entities. They allow you to
focus your power and release it. Think of the
way crucifixes are used to ward off vampires.
Yes, I've used a crucifix once or twice over
the years. I'm not a Christian anymore but the
symbology certainly has its uses.

James was working as a technical support
agent at Apple Computers. He had a dream of
becoming a librarian which never
materialised. He wasn't happy in his job.
Being a slave to the god of information
technology was not something he bragged
about. But he was suited to the role. He was a
natural problem solver. Plus, he was a nice
guy. He knew how to treat people. And his
work proved to be useful to the business. The
god of information technology was growing
more powerful by the day. James was on the
inside. It wasn't that this deity was the enemy.
It just needed to be watched. And James was
well placed to do this.

What about myself? Well, I was still on the
dole. I hate that word. Dole. I really should
have the right to call it a magician's allowance
or something like that. We don't make any
money from this business. And it is a
business. Some people would say it's just a
lifestyle. But it's not. It's a living. A lot of
what we do is ghost busting. You know how
the song goes. But it's not always as simple as

that. When you get involved in the occult there is always business to be taken care of and it's not always plain good versus evil. And disputes can't always be resolved through words. Believe me. I've been involved in many a battle and skirmish over the years. Mostly caught in the crossfire. Anyway. To that day in the Summer of 1999.

Back then, the three of us were living in the same apartment. It was on the second floor of an old house on the Northside of the city. Near the Cathedral. Which meant we were also near the city centre. It was a nice apartment: modern, spacious, clean. It had two bedrooms which made it affordable. We had some great times in that apartment. There was the time James bought a home brew kit and nearly blinded us all with the beer he made. Too much sugar in it.

Another time, we were having a party and Billy, the guitarist in my band, went to the toilet and returned a few minutes later, bollocks naked, and sat down at the end of the leather sofa, crossing his legs. You know. The usual shit a gang of twenty somethings gets up to. But mostly I remember just sitting on the sofa with a beer in my hand and Miranda beside me. Just listening to our favourite music and talking. Some of the best days of my life were spent in that apartment.

You might have noticed that I didn't mention anything paranormal. Well, that's just the way we like to keep things: there is public and there is private. Or at least we try to keep things that way. So, you see what I mean when I say it's not a lifestyle?

It was a Friday afternoon. The sun was powerful, making the living room hot and stagnant. There was no noise except for the ticking of the electric clock on the wall and distant traffic horns. I was lying supine on the leather sofa, smoking. James was in the armchair, his palms down on the arm rests, a look of concentration on his face. I had seen that look before. It was a habit he had picked up after that first encounter with the supernatural in his bedsit a few years before. He said it was called 'insight' meditation. It was used to focus the mind and attain higher mental power. Miranda was standing, leaning a shoulder against the jamb of the archway that separated the kitchen from the living room. The day was wasted on us. I made my thought known.

'Well, what do you suggest we do?' Miranda said.

'I don't know. Go for a walk. Hug a tree. Pick flowers.'

'I'd never have you figured for a hippy, Steve.'

'Hey, the 90s is the 60s upside down,' I said.

'Give me a cigarette,' she said.

I got up and liberated a cigarette for her. 'What do you think we should do?'

'Why don't we just go out and walk and see where it takes us. We haven't done that in a long time.'

'What do you say, James?' I said.

'Too hot,' he said, still meditating on some inner object.

'The man with the brains says it's too hot. Think of something else.'

'We could go to the beach,' Miranda said.

'What do you think, James?'

'Too crowded.'

'The man says it's too crowded. Think of something else.'

'Oh, this is ridiculous,' she said and turned around, walking into the kitchen. I heard the electric kettle come to life with a low expiration. As it grew, Miranda came into the living room and picked up the empty mugs from the coffee table, the cigarette between her lips. I looked at the rings the mugs had left behind them. Then I looked under the glass top at the books and magazines piled neatly on the wooden shelf below. I picked up the first book. It was an art book about Salvador Dali. I opened it and thumbed through it.

'God, I hate Salvador Dali,' I murmured and tossed the book back on the pile. Miranda returned with a kitchen cloth and wiped the surface of the table clean. I remained in a state of lassitude and James continued to meditate. She went back into the kitchen and returned again with a steaming mug of coffee. I made way for her on the leather sofa and she sat down.

Nothing was said for a while. She sipped, I smoked, and James concentrated.

Then, suddenly, James broke out of his meditation and said, 'Let's get pissed.'

Miranda laughed.

'You've been meditating over an hour, James. Is that the best you can do?' I said.

'Yeah, let's go on a good, old fashioned pub crawl. We haven't done that in a long time,' he said.

I looked at Miranda. 'What do you think?'

She nodded. 'He's right.'

'How are we for funds?' I asked her.

'No need for that. I'm talking about an astral pub crawl. Starting at The Dionysian,' he said.

'What do you think?' I said to Miranda again.

'Yeah, what the hell.'

'It could be dangerous,' I said. 'We might come across some enemies.'

'That's all part of the fun,' James said. 'And, anyway, if we stay here, we are in danger of losing our minds.'

'True,' Miranda said and sipped on her coffee.

'Ok. All those in favour of a psychic pub crawl raise your hands,' I said.

All three of us did.

'Motion carried,' I said.

'We'll need to bring some supplies. Food and that. Steve, give me a hand,' Miranda said. So, we went into the kitchen and sorted out some food and other provisions. We put them into my old ruck sack.

I put on my trench coat. 'Are we all ready?' I said, patting the pockets. 'I'm going to need more cigarettes.'

'Do you really have to wear that?' Miranda said.

'I've an image to keep up,' I said. I remembered a time when Miranda liked the trench coat. It was one of the things that attracted her to me. How things change.

The Dionysian was a classical themed pub that was accessed via the Crawford Art Gallery. It was James' favourite bar. We accessed it by entering the first room of the gallery which, back then, contained copies of classical Greek statues. The Apollo Belvedere. The Discus thrower. The Laocoon. We just went to the end of the room and passed through the wall into The Dionysian.

It was really like any other bar except for the clientele. There were quite a few satyrs about. Some nymphs. There were also men in togas: philosophers, poets. Behind the bar stood a centaur, drying pint glasses with a cloth. And there were people from our plane there too. We weren't the only ones to have a key to the otherworld. Some people used the mystic arts, like us. Others just had natural talent. And some came across it purely by accident.

So, we found a table in a nice cosy corner and I went to the bar to order some beers. I greeted the barman. His name was Troy.

'Can I have three pints of Murphy's, please?'

'Coming up,' he said and turned around to get the pint glasses. The area behind the bar was spacious to allow for Troy to get around with his four horse's legs. But aside from that he was a regular Irish barman: stout, pleasant, civilised, and laconic. As he placed a glass under the tap, I looked around me. There was only one other person at the area of the bar I was in. The owner of the pub: the young god, Dionysus. He had a dark face and dark, curling hair. His lips were crimson as he sipped wine from a wine glass. He was drunk but was still reasonably coherent and intelligent enough to hold a conversation. I didn't know him very well. But we were acquainted. He recognised my face.

'How are you?'

'Good, thanks. How are you?' I said.

'I'm okay. Considering.'

'Considering what?' I asked.

'Considering the fact that I'm dying.' I looked at him and there was not a trace of irony or archness on his face. I didn't know what to say.

'Ah never mind, eh?' Dionysus said.

'What do you mean by dying?' I said.

'Nobody goes to the theatre anymore.'

'Yeah, I know. It's a shame,' I said.

He looked at me for a few seconds, then got up off his bar stool and came over to me, keeping an arm on the bar for support. There was a powerful smell of wine and tobacco from his breath.

'I've seen you before. You're John Summoner.'

'Afraid not. Steve Jones is my name. But I am one of the trench coat Brigade. You're the God of wine, yeah?' I said.

The young god moaned in complaint. 'Wine, wine, wine. That's all people ever think of. They don't know that I'm also in charge of theatre.'

'I see.'

'Nobody goes to the theatre anymore,' he repeated. 'They're all enamoured with cinema. What an anti-social medium. It's almost as anti-social as reading. The people need Tragedy. They need drama. You know what drama is really about?'

'Conflict?'

'No. It's about saying what is left unsaid in society. Breaking the veneer of civilisation. It's about release. Understand?'

'Yeah. Sort of.'

'So, what do you do? For a living?'

After giving it some thought, I smiled at him and said, 'Ghost busting.'

He returned the smile. 'Aha. I think I like you. Want to stay here and drink with me?'

'Sorry. I'm with company,' I said.

'That's ok. That's cool.'

'You can join us if you want.'

'No. I'm socially awkward. It's why I drink so much,' he said and smiled again. It was a curly, cheeky sort of smile. Then he slouched back to his bar stool, sat down, and sipped some more wine. He gazed into the middle distance. It was as if we had never spoke. I felt kind of sorry for him.

The table we had picked was indeed cosy. It was by a natural fire in a natural fireplace: a nice little corner. I brought over the three pints of Murphy's, walking carefully so as not to upset them. When I had landed them on the table, I sat down beside Miranda. James was opposite. I sipped from my pint.

'I just had a word with the owner,' I said to James.

'Yeah? How is he?'

'He says he's dying.'

James laughed. 'Don't worry. He'll bounce back. He always does.'

'We were talking about drama.'

'Is that right? Must have a word with him later. If he's still in a generous mood.'

I elbowed Miranda and said to her, 'The man socialises with gods. What can you say?'

'Everything ok here, folks?'

Me and Miranda looked up. There was young man with blonde, curly hair and radiant blue eyes. There was a placid expression on his face.

'Yes fine, thanks,' I said. James turned to look up at the man also.

'If you need anything, just let us know,' he said and walked away.

'Apollo,' James informed us in a hushed tone. 'Dionysus' brother.'

'Does he own the pub as well?' Miranda asked.

'Yes. They are brothers. They don't get along, though.'

'Seemed kind of strange,' Miranda said.

'Yes, he is a bit.'

'Hey, let's break out the cigarettes.'

I reached into my coat pocket and produced a fresh packet of Silk Cut Blue. I opened it, drew out a cigarette and then placed the carton on the table. Miranda was trying to give them up and having little success. Which was why she was bumming them off me.

'You're going to need this,' a voice said.

We looked up and there was Apollo again. He was holding a large gleaming glass ashtray. He placed it in the middle of the table and was gone again before we could thank him.

'So, this is your favourite pub, James,' Miranda said.

'Yes, well, you know, the Greeks started it all. Western Civilisation,' he said and picked up my zippo lighter. He opened it and thumbed the wheel, producing a flame. 'Greek fire they call it,' he said and smiled. He closed it again, snuffing out the flame and looked at the engraving on the silver coated case. There was a circle with a triangle inside it. 'This a new one, Steve?'

'Yep.' It was a symbol Miranda had designed for me. To help protect the three of us if we ran into any trouble. I got it done at this tobacco and whiskey shop, off Patrick Street. Real swanky place but they did great customised engravings.

'And who was it who saved civilisation in the Dark Ages?'

Me and Miranda looked up again. There was a tall man with a ruddy face and a shock of white hair. He looked down at us avidly. He wore a blue T-shirt and a pair of plaid trousers. 'Who was it but the Irish?'

James turned around and looked up at the man. 'Ogma!'

'James,' the man said and smiled. It was a beaming, powerful smile.

'Guys, this is Ogma,' James said. 'Have a seat, my friend!'

'As long as I'm not interrupting?'

'No, we just got here,' James said.

He sat down beside James. 'How are things with you? Still reading and writing, I hope?'

'Ogma is a God of writing and learning, but also eloquence,' James informed us. 'Yes, my silver-tongued friend. I am still most definitely at it.'

'Excellent!' Ogma said

'What was that you said about saving civilisation?' I asked him.

'Don't you know your history, boy?' He had a slightly amazed expression on his ruddy face.

'A bit…well, not really…' I said.

'It was Irish monks who rescued the classical authors as the libraries of Europe burned under the hand of the heathen. And it was Irish monks who restored those works and planted the seeds of the Renaissance. Yes, we saved Classical civilisation. What a pity we couldn't save our own,' he said.

'What do you mean our own?' I asked him.

He looked even more amazed. 'Gaelic Civilisation. That's what I'm talking about. Once one of the finest pearls of Europe. What a terrible thing it is for a nation to lose its tongue!' He looked over my shoulder into the middle distance as melancholy took hold.

We looked at each other, not knowing what to say.

'At least we still have the music,' I said, in an attempt to cheer him up again.

'Yes. That's right, boy. We still have the music. But I fear that is going too. I hear young people talking on the streets these days and they sound more like Yanks than Irish.'

'Yes, but I mean traditional music,' I said. 'You know, traditional Irish music.'

'Yes. And that might be all that's left if things keep going as they are going.' He continued to look over my shoulder, his face a mask of melancholy. Then he looked at me again and said, 'But don't mind me. I'm just in love with the old ways. You are young and you need to look ahead. The future is more important than the past.'

'The future's uncertain. Especially with this new god, Mac, on the scene,' I said.

Ogma looked avid again and said, 'Yes, you're right. I don't know what to make of him. He's been kind to this country. There's no doubt about that. But I'd worry about the ramifications for society.'

'What do you mean?' Miranda said.

'I'd worry that he might be turning us into a nation of introverts. Imagine that! The Irish! A nation of introverts!'

'I don't think that will happen,' James said. 'A revolution is coming, that's for sure, but it won't be the last. We're all caught up in this, including Mac. Nothing can stop it. Let's just hope that things change for the good. That things fall on the right side.'

'I can't help but feel a bit responsible, though, James,' Ogma said. 'As a God of writing.'

'Ogma invented Ogham,' James explained to us.

'I see,' I said.

'What's with the club?' Miranda asked him. Ogma had placed a small wooden club on the table before him when he had joined us.

'This?' He picked it up and shook it slightly. 'Sometimes, the only language people understand is violence. If you want to get the message home, a good whack on the head is required. A last resort, you understand.' He sighed and said, 'Haven't used it in a long time.'

'Surely that's a good thing?' Miranda said.

'Yes, of course! But I sometimes miss a good scrap. Now, if you'll excuse me, I'm going to the bar to get a pint of Guinness.' He got up but left his club on the table.

'Seems like a nice fellow,' I said.

'I like him,' Miranda said.

'Yes. Be nice to him and he might tell us a story,' James said.

'Is he really a god?' Miranda asked.

'Yes, of course,' James said. 'Why do you ask?'

'I don't know. He seems a bit melancholy to be a god. I thought gods and goddesses were all, you know, happy and blissful.'

'You obviously haven't met Dionysus, then,' I said.

When Ogma returned with his pint of Guinness, he was once more beaming. He sat down and sipped from the glass. 'Mmmmm. I had a terrible thirst on me. I walked all the way from Wexford.'

'Today?' Miranda said.

'Yes. Glorious day for a walk,' he said.

'You must be a fast walker,' she said.

'Not fast. I just take very long strides. And I swing my club. Gets me to where I want to go.'

'Do you travel much?'

'Not as much as I used to. I miss the trees. This island was once a green blanket of trees. There is nothing like a walk through a forest on a warm, summer's day.'

'Tell us a story, Ogma,' James said.

'A story? Hmmm. What would like to hear?'

'We don't mind. Anything. Isn't that right, guys?' Myself and Miranda nodded.

'Hmmm. Let me think.' The god looked over at the fire. He looked completely impassive for a few seconds before he returned his eye and said, 'Here's a little story for you. Have you heard of the Ancient Greek poet, Homer?'

'Yes, of course,' James said. Miranda and I nodded again.

'Tradition has it that Homer composed *The Iliad* first and *The Odyssey* next. What if I was to tell you that *The Odyssey* came first, and *The Iliad* was a prequel? Also, most people consider Homer to be a man. In fact, Homer was two people: a woman and a man. The woman wrote *The Odyssey* and the man wrote *The Iliad*. There you have it. Two of the best kept secrets of the Ancient World.'

'How do you know?' Miranda said.

'Well, as I say, I love to walk. I love to travel. People say I'm a God of learning. Travelling is the best education you can get. If you really want to find the Universal, you have to go out there and discover it.

'So, the year was sometime in the eighth century BC. I was on a tour of Europe. Like Ireland, Europe was mostly forested back then. You should have seen it, man! It was such a beautiful continent. The paradise of the World. And the paradise of Europe had to be Greece. (With Ireland coming in a close second.) When I had explored the mainland, I switched from walking to boating, in order to see the hundreds of islands off the coast. So, there I was. Island hopping in Ancient Greece. The air was so clear then! Inhaling it would give you a powerful feeling in the brain. It's no wonder that it became the

birthplace of Western Civilisation. These
islands were mostly rugged but idyllic at the
same time. A nice combination, I think. The
beaches were pristine: blinding white sand
and blue sea that was as transparent as the air.
The mountains were harsh but in them were
pockets of greenery and glens, often serving
as places for temples to the gods. And, of
course, there were rivers, which were home to
the maenads. There was also arable land
which was used for cultivating orchards:
orange, citrus and olive. That's if memory
serves me right. The old brain is not as good
as it used to be, so forgive any errors I make.
I met many interesting people on my tour, a
lot of whom were gods or deities. They were
a nice bunch too, the Greek gods. Laid back
but also sociable. Just like the people. Hard to
believe they would spend so much time and
energy warring with each other.

'So, there I was in my little currach,
having a grand time exploring these islands.
As I say, in my travels I met many Greek
deities but the one who was most friendly was
undoubtedly Hermes. He often appeared to
me, either on land or sea, just to check up on
me. Like me, he loved to talk. I suspect he had
a soft spot for barbarians. Or perhaps he had
me figured for a Hyperborean. Whatever the
reason, he took it upon himself to watch out
for me but also to guide me and inform me
about the islands and their inhabitants. And I
trusted him. There were some islands he
warned me not to explore and I followed his

advice. But I didn't need to explore them as he would tell me everything about the land and its inhabitants. Between my own adventures and Hermes' stories, I built up a considerable store of knowledge about the islands of ancient Greece.

'So, I was approaching Asia Minor, the land you would call Turkey, and this would mean the end of my sojourn. There was one island left to explore: the island known as Chios. It was quite a large island, so I expected a lot of beautiful scenery and people. I was in my currach, approaching the land when Hermes appeared in my boat. He sat opposite me on the prow as he was accustomed to do. He had classic good looks and wore a kind of robe that he wrapped around his torso. His feet were adorned with little wings. He sat there, rubbing his ankles.

"It's been a busy day, my friend," he said, by way of explanation. I continued to row toward the shore. "So, you are now approaching the island of Chios," he said. I nodded silently in return. Even as a God of eloquence I know when to keep quiet. It's a good way to learn. "The inhabitants are Ionian, which means they are civilised. They have a king. You don't have to worry about him. It's his daughter that you must concern yourself with."

"Why?" I said.

"Because she's just discovered a new technology. A very powerful technology called 'writing'."

'Now, as you know, I'm a God of writing. But you have to consider that this was hundreds of years before I invented Ogham. So, I was in the dark, so to speak.

I gave Hermes a blank look and he said, "It's actually not that new. It's just that it was lost for a few centuries. This technology allows you to record words, poems, and stories, by using symbols. So, there is no need to memorise them."

"I see," I said.

"She is having trouble with it. She wants to write poetry. Epic poetry. But she doesn't know where to begin. I was thinking you could help her, being no minor poet yourself?"

"I see. What's her name?"

"Helena," he said.

"I'll see what I can do."

"She lives close to the shore, in a small palace, made of wood and stone. She is something of a recluse."

'When my currach had beached, we both got out. Hermes held his hand out and we shook hands. "I'll be seeing you again, hopefully. But not for a while," he said.

"Thanks for looking after me, lad. Maybe you could visit my part of the world some time and I could show you around. There's a lot of similarities between our peoples."

"I'd like that," he said. Then he flew away so fast it was almost like he had just disappeared into thin air.

'So, I was on my own again. I dragged my boat up to the trees that lined the far side of the shore. Then I dove into them, eager to explore. It wasn't long before I came to what I assumed to be Helena's palace. I don't remember much about it but I remember very vividly when I first saw her. She was sitting on the steps that led to the entrance, looking bored off her tree but, even so, she was a very beautiful looking young woman. Her hair was blonde and, unlike the other women I had seen on my voyage, it was unadorned and free flowing. She put me in mind of some of the women back home. She wore a chiton that was dyed a ruby-red and leather sandals. When she saw me, she raised her eyebrows.

"Hello, stranger," she said.

'I was surprised by her laidback attitude. It was almost as if she were expecting me. But the truth is, those were peaceful times and she probably thought she had nothing to fear from strangers.

"Hello," I said. "Hermes tells me that you are struggling with a new technology called writing?"

"You can say that again," she said.

"Maybe I can help you?"

"Do you know how to write?"

"No. But I know how to compose poetry. Maybe we could learn from each other."

'She seemed to ponder this for a moment.

"Maybe we could. Come on inside," she said. Once more I was struck by her easy-going attitude. I actually feared for her. No matter how peaceful the times are, a woman alone is always vulnerable.

'Once inside, she showed me some of her writing. She explained the symbols of the letters. She explained words and sentences. I was amazed. Then she asked me my name and proceeded to write it down on the papyrus she used. I was deeply impressed. "This is a form of magic, surely," I said.

"Yes, it is. I agree," she said. "I just can't seem to get it working for me. I want to write a long poem. A very long poem about the adventures of a man I call Odysseus. He is returning home from a great war in a place called Troy. It will be all about his fantastic adventures."

"I see. How long were you planning on making it?" I asked.

"Over 10,000 lines of Dactylic Hexameter."

"Crikey. That's a long poem alright. You'll probably spend the rest of your life writing it."

"That's ok. I plan on living a long time," she said.

"I can believe it. There is something about the air here."

"So, tell me about yourself."

'And that was how it began. I told her about Ireland and something of my life there. She seemed interested enough. It was when I started telling her about my recent island-hopping adventures that she became really interested. I made a fine concoction of biography, history, and legend, much of it having been learned from Hermes. She started writing almost straight away. It was just after we became lovers. Indeed, I would talk most just after we had coupled. I would lie there, and it seemed to flow right out of me. She would lie with her head propped on one hand, listening intently and in the morning, she would get up early to write. She was the first real writer I ever met, and she was good at it. Real good. In fact, she was a genius. And I don't use that word lightly.

'So, that's the story of how I inspired and informed, to some degree, the writing of *The Odyssey*. The Iliad, on the other hand, I had no hand in writing, even though I have been involved in many a war over the ages. Helena had a son and she named him Homer and it was he who wrote the prequel to *The Odyssey*. The epic poem of war.

'Did I feel used? Yes, I did. You could argue that she immortalised me but how do you immortalise an immortal? And even if I weren't immortal, the name of the hero is Odysseus not Ogma. And that makes all the difference. Everyone knows the name Odysseus. Who knows the name Ogma, besides scholars and magicians like yourselves? But I did get something out of it. I inspired her but she inspired me too. If it wasn't for her, I probably wouldn't have invented Ogham several centuries later. You might say that's a long time but for an immortal like me it is but the wink of an eye.

'Now, you are both looking at me with a question in your eyes and I think I know what that question is. Was I the father of Homer? The answer is no. He was begotten by some minor river deity, I believe. That's what I heard anyway. But, even so, I know it for a fact. Because I am sterile.'

We looked at him for a moment with a mixture of awe and pity, not knowing what to say.

'It's no tragedy. Why would I need children when I'm an immortal? Besides, us gods tend to be terribly irresponsible parents.'

'So, why wasn't Helena recognised? I mean as the author of the Odyssey? Why did Homer get all the praise?' I said.

'Ah, Steve, that, my friend, can be answered with one word,' Ogma said.

'Patriarchy,' Miranda said and Ogma nodded.

'They can't keep it secret forever, though,' the god said.

We fell silent. All that could be heard was the sound of the fire nearby. Ogma took a deep draught of stout and then put down his glass and nodded at us, silently, almost gloomily.

'So, have you done any writing yourself?' I asked him.

'Not for a very long time. It is usually our role to inspire writing rather than do it. I mean, do you know of any gods of writing who actually write?'

'James Joyce? Samuel Beckett?' James said.

'Aha,' Ogma said and laughed. 'They might write like gods but they are not immortal. Except through their works, of course.'

The mood cheered, the talk flowed and so did the beer. It's amazing the amount of conversation that can be had with only four people. I knew it was going to be a legendary crawl even at that early stage. There was this buzz in the air but there was also a kind of blissful thrumming inside. In the chest. Partly induced by alcohol but also by the thrill of being young and free.

I found myself talking to Apollo. He had pulled up a stool. He was quite a bright fellow. I noticed he wasn't drinking.

'Do you take drink?' I said to him.

'No, I prefer to keep a clear head. This place isn't going to run itself.'

'Are you really Dionysus' brother? You seem so different.'

He sighed and said, 'Yes. He's my brother.'

I sensed he didn't want to talk about his brother, so I changed the topic.

'We were talking about *The Odyssey* earlier. Do you know it was written by a woman?'

Apollo shook his head and said, 'That's not true.'

'How do you know?' I said.

'Because I was there when Homer wrote it. And Homer was most definitely a man.'

'That's not how Ogma tells it.'

'Ogma is wrong. I'm the God of epic poetry. I'd know.'

'He also says *The Odyssey* was written before *The Iliad*.'

'Not true.'

'Why would he lie to us?' I said.

'I don't know. But the facts are the facts.'

I didn't want to call him a liar, so I said, 'Maybe it's all about what you choose to believe. Or who you choose to believe.'

'I suppose so. But the historical facts are that *The Odyssey* was written by a man after he had finished *The Iliad*.'

Apollo then stood up, picked up the ashtray and left with it, without another word. I sensed that I had offended him. When he returned with a clean ash tray, I looked up at him and smiled but he was not a happy camper.

There was a lull in the conversation. A happy lull. We looked at each other with smiles in our eyes.

'So, where to next?' James asked.

'How about the Glade? You know. By the old church on North Main Street?' I said.

'Yes, I love the Glade. Let's go there,' Miranda said.

James nodded and looked at Ogma. 'Want to come along?'

'Er, no. I'm too old for pub crawls.'

'How can that be when you are immortal?' James said.

'I don't want to slow you down. No, today is for you,' Ogma said.

'All those in favour of having Ogma along, raise your hands,' James said. The three of us raised our hands. 'Motion carried. You're coming with us. Whether you like it or not.'

The old church on the North Main Street that I mentioned is a tall, Gothic style church called St. Peter's. The walk there sobered us up a little, but I still had a nice, mellow afternoon beer buzz going. We didn't talk much. Our spirits were high. Miranda kept grabbing my arm and looking at me and laughing. We got some strange looks from passers-by. Probably because of Ogma and his club, I reckoned. Then I realised that they wouldn't be able to see Ogma. They probably just thought we were on drugs or something.

When we had turned down the North Main Street, a young man in a tracksuit pants and plain white t-shirt stopped us, asking for a cigarette. I gave him one and he said, 'Ta. You look like you're having fun.'

'We're on a pub crawl,' I said.

'Is that right?' There was something familiar about the young man. I had seen his face before. Just couldn't place it. 'Where you headed for next?'

'The Glade. You probably wouldn't have heard of it,' I said.

'Why is that?'

'Uh, it's not of this world,' I said and laughed.

'Don't mind him,' Miranda said, elbowing me in the arm. 'We're going to the Thirsty Scholar. We're students,' she said.

'Oh, I see,' the young man said, lighting the cigarette with a zippo. 'What are ye studying?'

'Arts,' Miranda said.

'Must be handy with a paint brush so, yeah?' I couldn't tell if he was joking or not. 'I'm in a theatre company, myself. Called Graffiti. You ever heard of us?'

I was taken aback. I had him figured for a 'whacker'. Which meant an unemployed, uneducated young man from the Northside.

'Uh, the name does sound familiar,' I said.

'We're doing *The Tempest* in the Cat Club at the moment. I'm playing Caliban,' the young man said.

'I love that play,' Miranda said, softly.

'Come along some evening. We're playing all next week. Should be fun,' the young man said.

'Thanks. We might just do that,' I said.

'Enjoy yer pub crawl,' he said and walked away with a swagger, smoking the cigarette I had given him.

We came to the church. It was a tall, intimidating building. Very well designed and built but it had a dark cast to it. As if it had recently taken a beating from a storm. We entered, still in high spirits. Some people would have frowned on us, I suppose but we knew that inside was access to one of the most popular watering holes in the psychic life of the city. The Glade.

Inside, it was dark and hallowed and very quiet. I became acutely conscious of my breathing and everyone else's. There was a strong smell of incense in the air. We walked down the central aisle and turned right at the end. There was a heavy wooden door, large and oaken, and we passed through it without opening it, into The Glade.

The Glade was just that: a glade in a forest. It was always bright with sunlight, as if the sun had stalled at around noon and never moved on. Everywhere you looked there were entities, sitting and lying about in the tall, sweet-smelling grass. Faeries, sprites, goblins, ghosts, and gods. They drank beer from large plastic cups, served by monks. The monks moved around the place making sure everyone was taken care of. All in all, it had the feel of a music festival, without the music.

A monk came and welcomed us. 'Have a seat,' he said, indicating the general area. He was a balding, good-natured fellow with a large paunch. He also drank from a plastic cup. 'My name is Kevin,' he said, with a blissful little smile.

So, we sat down in the grass and waited for a monk to come and serve us. Miranda smiled and looked about the place in a contented sort of way. 'I love it here,' she said and sighed. 'It's so peaceful. Peaceful and…golden.'

I laughed at this. She punched me in the arm.

A monk came with four cups. It was an impressive feat, being able to hold the four cups in his two hands and walk through the grass as well. We accepted the cups gladly. There was no choice at The Glade. All they served was mead. But it was good mead.

We sat there, enjoying the sun on our faces and the alcohol in our veins. There was a nice hum of conversation about the place. Maybe later we'd get a story or two, or even a song.

Ogma laid back on his elbow, put a leaf of grass in his mouth and said, 'So, this is your favourite, pub. I hadn't you figured for a Dark Ages kind of gal, Miranda.'

'How can you call this dark?'

'True. The last great flowering of Celtic Civilisation happened during this era. The *Book of Kells*, the Tara Brooch…and I'm not going to turn this into another history lesson, am I?' Ogma said and smiled.

We conversed quietly for a while, feeling blessed with the sun and the free beer. James and Ogma were in the middle of an animated discussion about Irish Mythology when I felt the call of nature. I got up and walked to the edge of the clearing. When I reached it, I opened my fly and started to urinate. As I did so, I whistled a part from the old Elton John song, *Goodbye Yellow Brick Road*. I became aware of another guy, unzipping nearby. He began to whistle the same tune. I looked over at him. It was John Summoner.

''Lo, mate,' he said.

'Uh, hi John,' I said.

'You having a good time?'

'Yes. The best.'

'Good. Are you coming to see me in *The Tempest* at the Cat Club next week?'

I remembered the guy who had bummed the cigarette off of me. 'That was you? I knew he looked familiar!'

'Yeah, that was me. I was testing you, wasn't I?'

'How did I do?'

'You failed. Twice,' he said. 'First, you let him know about this place. I don't know how many times I have to tell you. There is our world and there is theirs. It's not good to mix the two. It's better all round to keep them separated. Second, you were surprised to find he was an actor, weren't you? Appearances are deceptive. You need to remember that.'

'But it's not fair. I'm drinking, aren't I?'

'That's when you're at your most vulnerable. You need to learn to control your mind and your tongue.'

'Ok. Want to join us?'

'Not now, mate. I'll catch up with ye at Shakespeare & Co.'

'Shakespeare & Co.? Ok, I'll let the others know, then.'

'And one more thing. Don't whistle when you urinate. Your ear is terrible.'

I returned to the others, somewhat chastened but also a little miffed. Why did he have to show up, spoiling my good time? He had visited me on several occasions in the past, always unexpectedly, but this was the first time he had done it while I was drinking. It wasn't fair. And not only had he tested and failed me, but he had also arrogantly presumed to name the next stop on our astral pub crawl: Shakespeare & Co. And, as if all this wasn't enough, he had insulted me by saying my ear was terrible.

'You ok?' Miranda asked.

I was about to tell her about Summoner when a buzz suddenly started up and began to go around, growing louder by the second. Something or someone was happening. We looked up. Yes, it was the storyteller: Beard. He was a very tall fellow with a long, silken, golden beard. His eyes were fierce but in a nice way. He wore a pair of combat trousers and a plaid shirt. He strode over to a large, rectangular shaped stone, placed roughly in the centre of the glade. The stone had Ogham inscribed along its edges. He sat down on the stone and looked about him, putting a hand on his knee. While he did this, everyone got up and moved toward him. It was almost automatic. Or maybe ritualistic is the word. Eventually, the movement of people created a rough natural amphitheatre facing the storyteller. There wasn't one person who had ignored the call of this powerful personage. Even the monks were seated in the grass at the edges of the audience.

When everyone was seated and settled down, Beard looked at the audience for half a minute, milking the silence and the anticipation. There likely wasn't one person in the audience who would swear that he didn't look directly at them, eye to eye.

'So,' he said and smiled. There was another silence before he continued. 'Many of you will know that I often tell the exploits of Ireland's greatest hero, Cù Chulainn. Many of these are written in the great epic of Cù Chulainn, the *Tàin Bò Cùailnge*. But there are other tales about him that are not contained in this book. Nor are they written down in any other book. They are the untold stories of the Hound, and this is one of them.

'As you all know, Cù Chulainn was the greatest warrior Ireland has ever known. And, like most warriors, his fate was to die young. But there was a time when the Hound was troubled by this fate. When he turned his back on war and violence and all the misery it causes. But he found that fate cannot be avoided. This is the story of what happened.

'There was a battle between the men of Ulster, or the men of the North, whatever you wish to call them, and the men of the West of Ireland. It was a small battle, hardly more than a skirmish, but the men of the North depended on Cù Chulainn and his warp spasm to defeat the enemy. So, the Hound let the warp spasm take hold of him. Now, I've spoken about this warp spasm in many a session before this one but now I will describe it at length. The warp spasm was truly a monstrous thing to behold. A hideous, misshapen thing that often defeated the enemy before they had even unsheathed their swords.

'First, each of his organs and limbs violently shuddered. He then turned around within his skin until his feet, knees and shins were at the rear and his heels and calves faced the front. The muscles at the side of his head expanded until they reached the nape of his neck, each protuberance the size of a baby's head. His face turned into a red bowl with one eye being pulled deep within his head and the other falling out across his cheek. His mouth distorted and the cheek fell away from his jaws until his gullet was exposed. His lungs and liver flopped into his mouth and throat, fiery flakes the size of the fleece of a ram exploding forth. His heart boomed loud in his chest, while above his head fire and mist coated the clouds with red. His hair was like the tangle of a red thorn bush, bristling up on his head in rage. Black blood rose from his skull like the smoke from a royal lodge welcoming home it's king.

'So, the men of the North slaughtered the men from Connacht and Cù Chulainn did most of the fighting himself. In fact, you could almost say that the men of Ulster were a one-man army. In the aftermath of the battle, as the Red Branch Knights (as they were also called) killed off the enemy dying and took care of their wounded, Cù Chulainn went to sit by himself at the edges of the meadow where the slaughter had taken place. A great shame darkened his mind. He thought of all the bloodshed he had caused in the past and waves of guilt passed through him, like midnight water. As he brooded, the other knights turned to watch him and they became fearful, as he had yet to come out of his warp spasm. He just sat there. A monstrous, brooding presence. After a while they left him. Afraid of what he would do to them and the people of Emain Macha if he returned in his current state.

'Cù Chulainn resolved to give up battle and cause no more bloodshed. But he found that he couldn't come out of his warp spasm. Such was the irony and misery fate had in store for him. He went back to Emain Macha and to his house where his wife awaited him. As soon as Emer saw him, she screamed and ran out of the house. Other people came to her aid and when they saw the Hound in his monstrous battle mode, they cried out and cast stones at him. Cù Chulainn knew that he would find no friends here. So, he left them.

'He resolved to go to the great healer of the gods, Dian Cecht, who resided in the South of Ireland. Dian Cecht was renowned throughout the land as a medicine man. If anyone could fix him up it was him. As the Hound travelled South, slouching in his monstrous form, he stayed off the major paths and roads, not wanting to be seen. This was out of shame but also out of a desire not to frighten innocent villagers and rustics. So it was that the greatest hero the land has ever known was reduced to a monster and a recluse. But fate had more misery in store for him.

'He found the hut of Dian Cecht near the province of Thomond. It was situated in a sequestered vale, so Cù Chulainn didn't have to worry about being seen by people. But as soon as the physician of the gods saw him, he knew that he would be of no help to him.

"Why can't you help me?" Cù Chulainn asked.

"Because the cause of your trouble is not physical but of the mind. I have no arts to heal it."

"I don't understand. Explain it to me," the Hound demanded.

"Alas, I can't. The mind is a mystery that no-one can solve."

"So, there is no-one who can help me?"

'The great healer stroked his beard slowly and softly. Cù Chulainn waited. "There is someone who might be able to help. One of my brethren, named Ogma. He is a god of learning and eloquence, but he was once a god of war," Dian Cecht said.

"I don't understand. How can he help me?"

"Ogma is a man of great cleverness. He is perhaps the cleverest of all the gods. If anyone can fix it, it's him."

"Where will I find him?"

"He lives in a crannog at the southernmost tip of Ireland. He is somewhat of a recluse, but he is friendly. Just tell him I sent you."

'So, Cù Chulainn made his way further south, again staying off the roads and pathways. As he travelled through the forest, he began to enjoy the sights and smells and sounds all around him. He began to understand why some men became reclusive. It wasn't such a bad life, he reflected.

'He came to Ogma's crannog. When the god saw him approach, he was filled with a mixture of pity and disgust, but he let him into his island hut. Cù Chulainn explained everything to him, including what Dian Cecht had said.

"I see. So, it's psychosomatic," the god said. "The mind acting on the body."

"Is there a cure for it?"

"Yes, there is. We must reverse it. Make the body act on the mind," Ogma said.

"How do we do that?"

"Simple. A single blow to the head with this should do the trick," said the god and he picked up a small wooden club and showed it to Cù Chulainn.

"You mean to strike me with that club?"

"Yes. On your temple."

The Hound shook his head and said, "I've given up violent ways. I'll not partake in another act of violence for as long as I live."

"You mean to turn me down?"

"Yes."

"It's the only way," Ogma said.

"That may be so. But I mean not to break my pledge."

"Ok. Come back to me if you change your mind."

'So, Cù Chulainn went on his way, with his slouching, hideous form. Once more he took to the forest and enjoyed a reclusive life. He walked the length of Ireland, with only birds for company. They sang to him and sometimes he would even sing back or whistle. He found a great peace in the forest and it gave him inner peace. He forgot his monstrous state and the way the people at Emain Macha had cast him out. He forgot his last battle. He began to forget all the battles he had been in. He became happier than he had been in a long, long time.

'One summer's day, as he walked through the forest, Cù Chulainn felt weary with the heat. He came to a small clearing which had a standing stone at its centre. He went to the stone and sat against it, resting himself. He looked around him in blissful contemplation. At that time the world had never seemed so perfect to the Hound. Then, suddenly, there was a loud fluttering noise in his right ear. A raven had landed on his right shoulder. It cawed loudly and Cù Chulainn found that he could understand what it said.

"Cù Chulainn, you must go back to Ogma and be healed and return to yourself," it said.

"I'm happier here."

"This is not your destiny. The gods have other things in store for you,"

"What if I resist?" Cù Chulainn said.

"You can't resist. You must return to Ulster and fulfil your destiny."

"I don't want to die young."

"Everyone dies young," the Raven said.

"You're pretty smart. For a raven," the Hound said.

"Yes, I am. That is why you must do as I say and return to Ogma."

'The Hound laughed at this, and it was the first time he had laughed in a long time. He felt something changing inside him. He no longer wanted to be in the forest. He wanted to see people again. So, he made his way back South to Ogma's crannog.

'The god welcomed him, again. He got him to sit down on a wooden stool as he was so tall Ogma couldn't reach his head while he was standing. Then the god delivered a swift, hard blow to the Hound's monstrous head. Almost instantly he was transformed back to his old self. He got up off the stool and thanked the god.

"So, does this mean I must go back to the North and become a great warrior again?" Cù Chulainn said.

"Yes, I'm afraid it does."

"You were a god of war once. Now you are dedicated to learning. Tell me, will there ever be peace on this island?"

"Yes, there will be. Very soon there will be a golden age that will last for centuries. Great art will be done, and civilisation will flourish."

"But I won't be around to see it," the Hound said.

"No, but you will never be forgotten. Your name will outlast all the names of all the heroes and deities of Ireland, including my own."

'So, the Hound returned to the North and Emain Macha and his destiny. And that is the tale of Cù Chulainn's brief life as a peaceful recluse.'

Beard nodded silently at the audience, again turning his head so that he could take in everyone. This was a sign that the story had ended. A great applause arose from the people. The storyteller broke out into laughter, slapping his knee with one hand.

When the applause had died down, he said, 'Someone get me a drink. That's thirsty work.'

Almost immediately the monk, Kevin, went to Beard with a large goblet, filled with mead. The storyteller accepted the cup and took a deep draught from it. Then he wiped his mouth and beard with the back of his hand and got up off the stone he had been sitting on. To my surprise and delight, he walked toward us. It was only when he stood before our little circle that I appreciated his great height. He must have been about 6'6".

'Sit with us, my friend,' Ogma said.

So, the storyteller sat down and introductions were made. I got a good look at the goblet he was drinking from. It was silver and bejewelled with emeralds and rubies. A very fine piece of work.

'So, is he really the cleverest person in all Ireland?' Miranda said to Beard, indicating Ogma.

'I'd say he is. What do you think? Would you believe it?'

'Yes, I think I would,' she said.

'You'd better believe it!' Ogma said jokingly, with a blade of grass between his lips. 'You're no slouch yourself either, of course,' he said to Beard.

The storyteller nodded in a humble sort of way. 'I do my best.'

'We're on a pub crawl. We just came from the Dionysian and next we're heading to Shakespeare & Co.,' I said.

'We are? Nobody told me,' James said.

'Me neither,' Miranda said.

'Yes. Who says so?' Ogma said.

'John Summoner. I met him when I was relieving myself. Before you came along,' I said, looking at Beard.

'Why should we?' Miranda said.

'Because he said so. He's never been wrong before and I trust him,' I said.

'I don't like him,' Miranda said.

'Yes, I know.'

'Who's this?' Beard said.

'English guy with trench coat and cigarette. A well-known, if not respected, magician,' Ogma said.

'I've never heard of him,' Beard said.

'Yes, you have. He's the joker, the rogue, the thief, the dancer…I could go on,' Ogma said.

'Come with us to Shakespeare & Co and you'll get to meet him,' I said.

'Excuse me, Steve. But haven't we still to decide on that?' James said.

'I think I'll pass. I'm not big on Renaissance pubs,' Beard said. 'A bit too strange and stuffy for me.'

'Is it just me or is there a pattern emerging here?' Ogma said.

'What do you mean?' James said.

'We seem to be following a story plotted on the evolution of Western Civilisation. I mean, first the Greeks, then the Dark Ages and now the Renaissance.'

'What about the Middle Ages?' Miranda said.

'I don't know. Maybe not interesting enough. Who knows? But there is a plot here. Believe me. I'd know. I'm the god of writing,' Ogma said.

'He's right,' I said. 'He's right. There is a plot here and Summoner is in on it. So, I say we go to Shakespeare & Co next.'

This was greeted with silence before Miranda said, 'Ok. I love Shakespeare. I just don't like the idea of being manipulated.'

'You're right. He is manipulative. But he's not manipulating us. There is something else at work here. A higher power maybe. I don't know. But it is bigger than Summoner. He's just a pawn, like us. And he knows it.'

'Ok, I'll buy that. Shakespeare & Co next it is, so,' James said.

'But you haven't been here that long, have you?' Beard said. 'Stick around for a while.

Enjoy the Sun. We might be having some music soon.'

As if on cue, someone began to sing. It was a woman's voice. High pitched. Ethereal. We turned our faces to the stone in the centre of the glade, where the voice was coming from, and saw a small, green creature standing on it and singing her heart out. It was Sing. She was naked, as usual, but her grassy hair was standing up as if she had received an electric shock. The song was in a plaintive air at first but turned joyful about halfway through. The lyrics were in French, except for the last line, which was in English: 'I pledge myself to you.'

When she finished, there was warm applause and she jumped off the stone, smiling and heading for our circle. She sat down next to Miranda and grinned at everyone, without saying a word. Sing hardly ever talked. She preferred to sing. She had shown up in my psychic life many times before this, but I still didn't know what her purpose was. If she had any. She liked Miranda: the two of them became fast friends when they had first met. Now they instantly dived into conversation as if picking up from a previous departure point. Miranda was the only person I knew who get Sing to talk.

I interrupted them to ask Sing if she wanted a drink She shook her head in negation. I had never seen her take a drink. I thought maybe she'd open up a bit after a few pints but…well, maybe later.

So, with the addition of Sing, that made a company of six. The conversation frothed and flowed. The Sun shone down from its zenith, and I felt that we too were approaching the zenith of our pub crawl. It just doesn't get much better than this. I looked at the faces of my friends and they were almost holy to me. This must be how a philanthropist feels, I thought to myself. Of course, it was largely down to alcohol but there was something else. Something infused in it. Something maybe divine. Ogma was the only deity present, so I looked at him and he looked back at me and winked. My introspective turn continued. I was 25. Still very young but no longer a spring chicken. I was old enough to know the effects of alcohol. But still young enough to be able to enjoy it. As you get older, alcohol becomes more a numbing agent than a bringer of joy. I think that that moment in The Glade was the last time I ever truly felt alcohol as a gift from the gods.

I thought about my meeting with the young god Dionysus earlier. He had said that drama was about breaking through the veneer of civilisation. He was right. How many times had I kept my mouth shut not just out of the fear of causing offence to another person but out of the fear of revealing myself? Of showing my hand? It's something we all do. Keeping things civilised. Of course, alcohol changes that. We all say things we regret when we are drunk. *In vino veritas*, as the saying goes. In wine there is truth. That is why the god Dionysus is the god of drama too. I wondered would we see any drama on our pub crawl? Would it break out amongst us? Or would we witness it? The next stop on our crawl would be the place for it. Shakespeare & Co. I liked Shakespeare but not as much as Miranda did.

I looked over at her. She was still wrapped up in a conversation with Sing. As they conversed, they nodded and gesticulated with their hands, as women do. I love Miranda. Sometimes I look at her and I can't help but feel amazed that she chose a nerd like me to be her boyfriend. Sometimes I get the urge to declare my love to the world. To sing it. Would that be a breaking of the veneer of civilisation? Probably. It would also be a breach of the peace as I'm a terrible singer. Yes, I love her. Does she love me? Yes, I think so. She tells me she does and one thing I know about Miranda is that she is no liar. But you can never truly know what goes on in another person's heart, can you? But I was lucky to meet her when I did. At the age of 20. Just the right time for it. Yes, there is no love like young love. What a lucky bastard I was.

Beard fished out a little baggie of cannabis from his breast pocket and started to roll a joint. He talked effortlessly as he rolled. When he had finished, he put it between his lips and lit up with a zippo. It was the longest and neatest joint I had ever seen. Rolled to perfection, with a roach at the top and a little twist at the end to prevent the cannabis from falling out. It was passed around and we each took two or three drags off of it, holding in a lungful for several seconds before exhaling. It was strong but not too strong. When it came back to Beard there was still a few pulls left in it.

Sing had accepted the joint and smoked it. It was clearly not her first time either. She started to sing, improvising some lyrics and a melody. From what I could gather, she was singing about a pet goldfish. I burst into laughter. Couldn't help myself. But she continued to sing, either ignoring me or not hearing me at all. I sat there with my head hanging, laughing almost to tears. When I looked up, I saw that Ogma was laughing too and Beard was looking at me, smiling, the joint in his mouth. Miranda was shaking her head in a resigned kind of way, but I suspected she wanted to laugh too. If Sing hadn't been such a good friend she probably would have. James was lying back, propped on one elbow, looking stoned.

When Sing had finished, she looked at me and said, 'You laugh at me because I'm different. I laugh at you because you are all the same.'

This shut me up. Ogma looked down at his beer, a little shamefaced. 'Sorry, Sing,' he said. 'It's just the cannabis.'

A monk walked by, and looked at us with a little frown and shake of his head. The place seemed to have quietened down. We resumed our conversation, but it didn't take long for us to realise that the monks weren't serving us anymore.

'I think we'd better leave,' James said. There was no need to take a vote on this one.

'Sorry folks. I guess it's my fault. They warned me about smoking weed. I'll know better next time,' Beard said.

We stood up, stretching our limbs and brushing the grass off our trousers. The hum of conversation in the glade picked up again. I asked Sing if she'd like to come with us to Shakespeare's. I did it out of guilt but also out of altruism. She smiled and accepted my offer. Then she took Miranda's hand and they walked ahead of me. We said goodbye to Beard. Kevin, the head monk, also came to say farewell and there was no admonition in his eyes. He said we were always welcome and I believed him. I shook his hand firmly.

Shakespeare & Co. was accessed via Waterstones book shop on Patrick's Street. We entered the store through the rear doors and almost immediately passed into a corridor of darkness before we found ourselves in the warm and comfortable environment of the public house. As Ogma had said, it was a Renaissance pub. Physically, it was like most any pub in Cork city, except for the books. There were hundreds of books, lining the walls, all of them hardback and none under a hundred years old, I reckoned. These books gave off a slightly mouldy smell that mixed pleasingly with the scent of beer and tobacco smoke. And, of course, there were the clientele. They were mostly characters from Shakespeare's plays, especially *A Mid-Summer Night's Dream* and *The Tempest*. There were one or two Pucks around the place and a flying fairy that could only be Ariel. In one corner sat Oberon and his wife, Titania, king and queen of Faerie. In another sat Prospero the magician and his daughter, Miranda. (Not Miranda, my girlfriend).

We found a nice spot to sit down at: a large, square oaken table to accommodate the five of us. There were words carved into the surface: Renaissance English but also Gaelic and Latin and even some Greek. Ogma went to the bar to get the drinks. I remembered what Beard had said about Renaissance pubs: too strange and stuffy. I could understand where he was coming from but this place did not feel that way at all.

'What do you think?' I said to Miranda.

She was sitting by Sing again. 'I love it,' she said.

Ogma returned with the drinks. We were on the stout again, except for Miranda, who was on the shorts. Southern Comfort with ice. Sing stayed sober. She seemed to have gotten over the incident with the song. But I suspected we wouldn't hear any more from her for the rest of the evening. Forgive but don't forget, as they say.

Ogma sat down opposite myself and James and sipped from his pint before indicating behind him. 'Look who's at the bar,' he said, in a low, reverential tone.

We looked over his shoulder. There, propping up the bar, were William Shakespeare and James Joyce, apparently far into a conversation. Joyce was talking and Shakespeare was listening, nodding his head intermittently.

'Now there's a dialogue I'd like to eavesdrop in on,' I said.

'Why don't you?' Ogma said.

'Maybe later.'

So, the drink continued to flow. And everyone talked with gusto. We seemed to be on the crest of another wave of pleasure. The conversation swirled and eddied about us. I was put in mind of a Jack Kerouac novel: everyone rapping away with a surfeit of energy and intelligence. But where was John Summoner? Don't get me wrong. I had no great desire to see him. But he had said he would be here. Never mind. I was sure he'd pop up again. I got up, intending to approach Joyce and Shakespeare. My plan was to just hover around near them, so that I could overhear a little of their conversation. When she saw me rise, Miranda asked me to get her another shot of Suds. Great! This gave me a good excuse. So, I went to the bar and ordered another Southern Comfort with ice. I stood near the two geniuses. Joyce, again, was holding forth. There were two pints of stout before them. Completely untouched and unspoiled. I won't record their conversation here as it is beyond my powers of recollection and I wouldn't be able to do it justice anyway, if I could recall any of it. All I'll say is that Joyce was waxing poetically and philosophically on the aesthetics of a fresh, untouched pint of stout, straight from the tap. The term 'undiscovered country' was used more than once. Again, it seemed like Joyce was doing all the talking. Strange to think of Shakespeare being silent. But there you have it. When I had heard enough, I returned to the others with Miranda's drink.

'Joyce is talking about the beauty of a pint of stout,' I said as I plonked myself down on the bench again.

'A pint of stout?' Ogma said. 'Two of the greatest minds of Western literature are talking about a pint of stout?'

'Well, it is a thing of beauty,' I said.

James, who had seemed to be well on his way to Drunk Country, spoke up. 'Within the particular is contained the universal,' he intoned, pronouncing every word carefully and raising his index finger for dramatic effect.

There was a moments silence before a general felicitous cheer broke out. Such a good line! Miranda and Sing clapped and Ogma beamed at him. 'Joyce said that,' James added before turning silent again.

The conversation moved on to other things.

I lit a cigarette and looked around me with frank pleasure. James wasn't the only one on the way to that country. We all were. But I still had a lot of mileage left in me. My right knee bounced up and down rapidly, energetically. I looked at Miranda. Her eyes were half shut and her head was nodding slowly as she talked with Sing. She looked up at me and our eyes met for a few seconds before she smiled and winked theatrically. Then she returned to her conversation. It was a kind of a disingenuous smile but I didn't mind. You couldn't win them all.

I looked over at Prospero and his daughter, the other Miranda. They did not look happy. The fabled magician was enveloped in gloom and his daughter looked plain fed up. I perceived the cause of their unhappiness straight away. They weren't drinking. So, boldly, I decided to get up and try to remedy the situation. I walked over to their table which was located in a corner of the pub. When I reached it, I stood there looking down on them, smiling in a way that I hoped wasn't too foolish. 'Can I get you a drink?' I said.

Prospero was a dark, tetchy looking man with a sharp goatee beard and a crew cut. He wore a long robe, black but trimmed with gold. Miranda, his daughter, was an apple faced youth with an abundance of glossy, curled orange-red hair.

She looked up at me and smiled broadly and courteously. 'Why, yes. I'll have a vodka and orange juice, please,' she said.

'We're fine,' her father said, overruling her.

'Where's Ferdinand?' I asked. I had read *The Tempest* a couple of times and had an idea of what happened in it. Miranda gets married to Prince Ferdinand and they all return to Milan. Prospero gives up his magical power for a return to political power.

'He's out drinking with his mates. Having fun,' she said, emphasizing the last word and giving her father an accusing look.

'Uh, ok. Is it ok if I join you for a while? I have many questions to ask you, Mr. Prospero,' I said, hoping that this would flatter him.

It seemed to do the trick. He sighed and said, 'Pull up a stool.'

So, I did and thanked him politely. 'Why aren't you drinking?' I asked.

'Is that all you want to know, boy?' he said in a stern voice.

'I was just curious,' I said, placatingly.

'I don't take drink. My daughter here is too young for it.'

Ah,' I said. Miranda looked at me, rolling her eyes. I looked back, smiling in a sympathetic sort of way.

'Cigarette?' I said, offering the packet to Prospero. He sighed again but took one. Then I looked at Miranda. She looked at her father.

'Go on,' he said and she plucked a cigarette, smiling triumphantly.

After lighting their cigarettes, I said, 'I'm a magician. Or, at least, I'm training to be one.'

'Very good,' Prospero said.

'I was hoping you could give me some advice.'

He sighed and said, 'I'm not much of a magician, boy. But I know a thing or two about power.'

'But you're one of the world's most famous magicians,' I protested. 'You must know something.'

'Have you read the play?'

'*The Tempest*? Sure, I have.'

'Not closely enough. If you really study the play, you'll find that it's Ariel, my servant, who performs most of the magic.'

I frowned at this.

'So, it's him you should be asking,' Prospero said and grinned. It was a dark, skeletal grin.

I considered this for a few seconds. 'Ok. I see. So, there's nothing at all you can tell me about magic?'

'Not really, boy. Except to say that it is a good thing to have it on your side. Now, ask me about power,' he said.

'What about power?'

'On the surface of it, it seems that all power is about the master and servant relationship. It's like a circle. There is no way of getting out of it. Round and round we go. But that's not real power. Real power consists in setting a person free.'

'That's it? That's all you have to say?'

Yes,' Prospero said, smiling enigmatically through a blue curtain of cigarette smoke. 'Disappointed?' he asked.

'I am a bit.'

'Ok, but just remember: I'm a fictional character. If you want to know more, go talk to my creator.'

'Are you kidding? Me talk to William Shakespeare? I wouldn't know what to say. Christ, I'd shit my pants! Apologies, Miranda.' She smiled and shook her head, dismissively. 'No, I think I'll go over to Ariel and talk to him for a bit.'

'Good luck. You're going to need it,' Prospero said and indicated behind me. I turned round on my stool and had a look. The fairy, Ariel, who I had recognised earlier was now sitting on a stool at the bar, his head resting on the counter, apparently wasted. I turned back to Prospero and his daughter.

'Thanks for the cigarettes,' he said.

'Yes, thanks. What's your name?' Miranda said.

'Steve. Steve Jones,' I said. 'Thanks for the advice. Here,' I said and liberated two more cigarettes from the packet and handed them to Prospero. He nodded in appreciation and approbation.

Then I stood up and turned around and approached the fairy at the bar. As I did so, I was conscious of my trench coat sustained in the air behind me and I hoped it had a dramatic effect. I was in my 'immortal' phase of drunkenness.

Ariel was a small creature dressed in a white habit. His wings were light and translucent, like a fly's wings and they rested flat against his back. His head was half hidden by his arms, which rested on the counter of the bar.

I shook his shoulder, tentatively. I could only see one eye lid and it opened. It was a strange eye, all green and gold. I found myself wondering was he really drunk or was he just resting. He closed his eye again after a few seconds. Once more I shook his shoulder. He moaned and raised his head and looked at me. His face was flushed and his lips were full. Yes, he was drunk. And I, being drunk too, tried to engage him in conversation.

'I want to learn about magic. Can you tell me about magic?' I asked.

'Want to learn about magic? I'll tell you about magic. It's a fool's game,' he slurred. His breath reeked of alcohol.

'Why do you say that?'

'Because it is,' he said, and laughed. It was a quiet, reedy kind of laugh.

'I want to know how do you do what you do?' I insisted.

'I do it because I'm a natural,' he said and laughed again, as if at some private joke.

'Prospero says that you are the real magician of *The Tempest*,' I said. He looked stupidly at the mirror on the far side of the bar. 'Prospero says that real power is about setting another person free. Just like he sets you free at the end of the play, right? Am I right?'

The fairy turned his face back to me. It was delicate but stubbled with a few days' growth of beard. A strange complexion. He looked me in the eye, as if mustering all his powers of lucidity. 'He said that?' he asked.

'Yes. He did,' I said.

He returned his gaze to the mirror. I looked at it and I could see his reflection: there was so much pain and despair there, it was tragic. I felt guilty about waking him up.

'Christ, what a planet,' he said in a curious, quiet voice that almost sounded sober. Then he lay his head down between his arms again and was gone.

I looked at him, feeling a bit crestfallen. I remembered what Prospero had said about talking to Shakespeare, his creator, but that was far too intimidating a prospect, even in my somewhat drunken state. So, resignedly, I turned around with the intention of returning to my friends. But I was stopped by the sight of Miranda, my Miranda, sitting alone on a barstool. She looked at me, her left elbow resting on the counter of the bar. In her right hand she held a glass of Suds. I approached her.

'Is everything ok?' I said, with awakening concern.

She laughed, her eyes half closed from drink. 'No, everything is most definitely not ok, Steve,' she said. Her voice was thick. I didn't know if it was from alcohol or impending tears or both. 'Pull up a stool,' she said.

'I'm ok. I can stand,' I said.

'No, you need to pull up a stool and sit down before you hear this. Really.'

So, I did. She looked at me through her hooded eyes and took a sip of her bourbon.

'What is it?' I asked. She continued to look at me. She was drunker than I thought. 'Oh, Christ! Don't tell me you're pregnant, Miranda. Please don't tell me you're pregnant!'

She shook her head in negation.

'Then what is it? It can't be that bad, Miranda. Unless…are you unwell? Do you have like a terminal disease or something?'

She laughed at this and took another sip from her glass. She seemed to be getting drunker while I was getting more sober. She shook her head again in negation.

'Stop laughing, Miranda! Tell me what it is?'

'I'm bisexual,' she said, at last.

Was I surprised? Yes, I was. In fact, I was speechless. But I have to admit I was somewhat relieved as well. I let out a long and steady exhalation. 'Are you sure?' I said, eventually.

'I'm sure,' she said.

'Ok. Ok. This is not the end of the world,' I said. 'We can get through this.'

'That's not all,' she said. There was no sign of laughter about her now. 'I'm seeing someone.'

'What!' I exclaimed. I looked at her, bewildered for a second. Then I felt a bolt of anger pass through me.

'Oh, Steve, I'm sorry! I'm so sorry! Please don't…'

'Who is it?' I demanded. She started to cry. 'Who is it?' I demanded again, my voice stern with the effort at self-control.

'It's Sing.'

'Sing!' I sighed deeply and my anger began to dissipate as swiftly as it had come upon me. It could have been worse. It could have been a guy. 'I should have guessed,' I said, dejectedly. 'You two are always together.'

'I'm sorry Steve.'

How long?' I said. I was now looking down on the wooden surface of the bar counter. It was polished and unmarked. Maybe I would remedy that later. A big ol' love heart split right down the middle.

'About six months,' she said.

I looked behind me at the others, sitting at the oaken table. Thankfully, they seemed oblivious to what was happening.

'You sure picked a shitty time to tell me,' I said. 'Now I'll never be able to get drunk.'

'I'm sorry, Steve.'

'Stop saying that. Stop apologising.'

'I wouldn't have been able to tell you sober. I had to get tanked up,' she said.

'So, do you love her?' I said and looked her in the eyes again.

'Yes, I do.'

'Ok, well that's that then. We're finished,' I said and got up off my stool. I looked out for the barman. I might not have been able to get drunk again but I sure as Hell was going to try.

'Steve!' she said. 'Please, Steve!'

'What? Please what?' I said, my voice rising again. 'What else is there to say?'

'I still love you, Steve,' she said.

I sighed again, looking at the far side of the bar and shaking my head. 'The plot thickens!' I said, sardonically. 'So, what do you want? Do you want me to be a part of some kind of weird sex triangle thing? Is that it?'

'I just thought…' She started to cry again.

'Thought what? That we could experiment?'

She turned her face away and continued to cry.

'Oh, stop crying,' I said, calm again. 'You'll ruin the whole friggin pub crawl.'

'I can't help it, Steve.'

'Have another drink,' I said, flatly. 'I sure need one.'

I sighed once more and sat down on the bar stool again. On the far side of the bar was another mirror, this one half obscured by bottles, decanters and glasses. I looked at it and was struck by how clownish I appeared. I almost laughed. It was comical.

'Do you still love me, Steve?' she asked.

'Yeah, of course I do. Stop being so pathetic. It doesn't suit you.' She went silent after hearing this. I caught the barman's eye and he approached. He was a tall man in a gaberdine, his face Neronian. I ordered a Suds with ice and a Powers, neat.

When our drinks arrived, we each took a sip. I continued to look in the mirror, contemplating how ridiculous I was.

'So, what now?' she asked eventually.

'What now? Let's just pretend this conversation never happened and get back to our pub crawl.'

'That's easier said than done.'

'We can talk more, tomorrow.'

She seemed happy with this. 'It's so good to have it out in the open,' she said.

'Just one more question,' I said. 'What does Sing want?'

'Sing? She's…uh…easy about it, I guess. She says as long as we can be together, she is happy.'

'I see.'

We returned to the others. They talked like nothing had happened but I could sense that they had guessed something was up between us. Miranda sat beside me. Sing, sitting opposite, looked at us with an expression that was half sheep and half imp. Her green body seemed to glow. I have to admit, I thought about the three of us in bed together and it kind of turned me on. Sing then gave me this horny kind of look, as if she knew what I was thinking, and I almost burst out laughing. Luckily, I managed to contain it. I didn't want to upset her again, even if she had stolen the love of my life. When she had first appeared to me a couple of years ago, she had said I would be seeing a lot of her in the future. Was this what she had meant? Was this to be her role in my life? Well, everything else in my life was weird. Why not this? It seemed like fate was determined to deliver me from a normal existence. I still felt a little angry and also a little envious. But there was something childlike about Sing that excused a lot of her behaviour. Yes, we would have to talk about it tomorrow. I would likely be hungover but red eyed or green eyed, it had to be resolved. It would probably end up with us splitting. That was the harsh reality I would have to prepare myself for. In the meantime, I numbed myself with alcohol.

To take my mind off it, I said, 'where to next, people?'

'We were just discussing that,' James enthused, apparently getting a second wind. 'If we are to let the plot take its natural course, the next stop on our journey is the Enlightenment. But I was saying we are free to choose. We can go where we like, now. What do you think Steven?'

'Hmmm,' I said and scratched my cheek. 'I really don't know.'

'Perhaps we can do a bit of both?' Ogma said. 'Perhaps we can follow the plot and do our own thing at the same time.'

'How?' James asked.

'Let's go the Liberty,' he said. This was greeted warmly by everyone. The Liberty was loved by all.

'But it's not exactly what you'd call an Enlightenment pub, is it?' I pointed out. 'I mean, the place is as dark as sin, for one thing.'

'Well, the Enlightenment wasn't such a good time for everyone,' Ogma reasoned. 'For people like us, it was really quite a dark time. The rise of empiricism and science undermined the imagination and those who live by it. Gods, monsters, storytellers, poets…So, a darkened pub would be kind of appropriate.'

'I'll buy that,' I said.

'Me too,' James said.

Miranda and Sing nodded as if in synchronicity.

And so, we left for The Liberty.

The Liberty was another Liminal: a place where the natural and the supernatural meet. So, we didn't have to go through another portal to get there. It existed on both planes. The pub situated on the South Main Street. Most of the naturals who drank there were students: young, openminded and able to keep a secret.

Inside was dark. Easily the darkest pub I've ever been in. And it was dirty. But I don't know of any other pub with as much character. There weren't many stools about, so most of us sat on empty beer kegs. The tables were mismatched and pulled about the place in a chaotic way. The floor was bare concrete, cracked and deteriorating in places. The only heat came from a small fireplace, tucked away in a nook. There was a large TV screen above the bar, showing mostly soccer matches, but it looked so out of place it was like an anachronism. Overall, it was like a building that was waiting to be condemned. And it was.

But, as I say, it had character, and it also served great stout.

We entered and there was the familiar rush of warmth and conversation fuelled by alcohol. We stood near the door, looking about us. It was a small pub so there wasn't enough seating to accommodate the five of us. I went to the bar to get in the drinks. The barman was a tall, very quiet individual with a laidback air about him. Giant ram's horns curled out of either side of his head. He seemed more interested in the football on the screen above him than the patrons. There was a man bent over the bar on his stool, also watching the football. He wore a jester's hat, the bells stilled and silent. In the murk, I could make out other creatures: a couple of satyrs lounged against one wall, their legs crossed, smoking. There was a Buddhist monk sitting at the far end of the bar, clad in a yellow mantle and perfectly bald. I looked in the direction of the fireplace and, lo and behold, there was John Summoner, beckoning to me.

He sat on a beer keg and was talking with Beard, the story teller from The Glade, and an old man who smoked a pipe. When I went to him, I recognised the old man as Dan Lee O'Brien. He was yet another paranormal investigator. Technically, he was the competition but we always got on well.

'What happened? You were supposed to meet me in Shakespeare's,' I said to Summoner.

'I got caught up. Sorry, mate,' he said. 'Just think of it as another lesson, yeah?'

'What lesson?' I said.

'That you're not the centre of the universe.'

'But you said to me you are only a work of fiction,' I complained.

'Yes, but as all writers know, fiction has a way of taking on a life of its own.'

'Why do you have an answer for everything?' I said. 'Aren't you ever stuck for words?'

'It's just me, mate. I've been bullshitting from the day I was born. It's gotten me out of some real jams over the years. So, why should I stop now?'

I sighed and nodded.

'Sit down with us. Beard here was about to tell a story.'

'What about the others?' I said.

'I don't think there is room for them, mate. Sorry.'

'Give me a sec.'

So, I walked over to my friends. 'Summoner's invited me to join him and hear another story from Beard,' I said. 'I don't think there's room for all of us. It's in the nook, by the fire. Dan lee O'Brien is there too. Sorry.'

'No need to apologise, my friend,' Ogma said.

'Yes. We don't mind,' Miranda said. As I told you earlier, Miranda doesn't have much time for John Summoner.

'James?' I said and looked at him. He was smiling blissfully.

'Go right ahead,' he said.

So, I returned to Summoner and took a beer keg for a seat. Dan lee offered me a puff off his pipe and I accepted. Beard seemed to be smoking another of his perfectly crafted joints.

'So, I've just been telling Beard that you are at the Enlightenment stage of your epic, astral, history hiking pub crawl,' Summoner said. 'And he has a story for you.'

'Yes. It's another untold tale of Cù Chulainn. An enlightenment tale,' Beard said. He drew long on his joint. There was an abstract look in his eyes. Then he focused his gaze on me and began.

'There came a time in Cù Chulainn's life when he was troubled by dreams and visions. Disturbing lightning images of men dying. Strange vehicles and strange weapons that spewed fire and thunder. The ground exploding and rivers of blood flowing and men crying out for their mothers. And the land smoking and reeking of death and piled up with corpses. Then the noise would die down and the visions would abate until he saw a single cross on a hill with a man crucified on it. The image flashed in Cù Chulainn's mind until all became silent. The Hound had no idea who that man was but, for some reason, it grieved him to see him there. He would recover but the image remained in his head. Troubling him. Accusing him. As if he were somehow responsible for that man's death.

'It was during these days that Cù Chulainn would go to a small river that flowed past Emain Macha. He found that being near water gave him respite from the dreams and visions but it also gave him a place to sit down and think.

'One day, the Hound fell asleep while he was sitting on the riverbank. It was a deep, dreamless sleep and when he awoke the land was bathed in golden twilight. He felt an inner peace that he hadn't felt in a long time. Then, something tapped him on the shoulder. He turned around and there was a man in a frieze coat, holding a walking stick in the air like a sword. The man was young and lithe, and he smiled at the Hound. Cù Chulainn perceived straight away that the man was blind, but he returned the smile, anyway.

"Who are you?" the Hound asked.

"My name is Raftery. Blind Raftery people often call me. I'm a bard. And you are Cù Chulainn, yes?"

"Yes, I am Cù Chulainn."

"Good. You're probably wondering where I come from. My clothes must seem strange to you. Well, I'm from the future. About

2,000 years into the future. Does that disturb you?"

"No. It should, I guess but it doesn't," the Hound said.

"Good. I'm here because we've been invited to a wedding, you and I."

'Cù Chulainn's face became animated when he heard this. "A wedding?"

"Yes. But this is no normal wedding, you must understand. It is a great wedding. A world-wedding. Not between nobles but divinities. We've been invited to represent Ireland."

"Where is it?" the Hound asked.

"It's in a great hall of kings, named Heurot. There will be a fair bit of travelling involved. We'll have to travel through time as well as space."

"I've never travelled through time before," the Hound said.

"Don't worry. Just hold my arm and we'll be fine."

"But you're blind."

"My eyes may be blind but the way we are going doesn't require that kind of vision. I can see here," Raftery said, tapping his forehead. "Does that make sense?"

"Yes, I guess so."

"Good. Then let's get going. We don't want to be late."

'So, they walked away from the riverbank, into the twilight. Soon it became dark and Cù Chulainn couldn't see a thing. "Just hold onto my arm," Raftery said.

"What kind of a wedding is this?"

"Like I said, it's a world-wedding. Something that doesn't happen very often."

"Where are we travelling to?"

"Denmark, a couple of hundred years from now. But you have to understand that this is just a meeting place. A crossroads. The guests will come from all over the space-time continuum."

"Why us? Why are we invited?"

"I'm not entirely sure. Maybe it's because you are Ireland's greatest warrior and I am Ireland's greatest poet."

"I don't understand," the Hound said.

"Nor do I. Maybe it will be revealed to us in time."

"Who is getting married?"

"It is a marriage of Heaven and Hell. Now stop your questions. You sound like a child."

"Is this something to do with the strange visions and dreams I've been having?" the Hound asked, ignoring the other man's imperative.

"What visions?"

"Strange warfare. And a man crucified on a hill."

"Oh, yes, it is very much to do with those things," Raftery said.

"Who is that man?"

"His name is Jesus Christ. He preached universal love. They crucified him."

"Because he preached universal love?"

"Yes. A religion was founded on his life and teachings. Terrible things were done in his name. Terrible things," the bard said. "This wedding is an attempt at restitution."

'Satisfied with this, Cù Chulainn fell silent.

'Soon they were walking through a meadow, approaching a huge hall with a thatched roof. The sun was out and the bright air was filled with bird song.

"Tell me, Hound. Do we approach Heurot?" Raftery said.

"Yes, I think we do. A great wooden hall with a thatched roof."

"That's it," the bard said. "Now is the time for you to guide me, Cu Chulainn."

'They came to the doors, which were closed. A woman was standing guard. She was dressed all over in armour. Her hair was so blonde it was almost white and her eyes were like sapphires. She held a flaming sword up, barring the way. "Declare yourselves," she said. Raftery responded:

"I am Raftery, the poet, full of courage and love.

My eyes without light, in calmness serene,
Taking my way by the light of my heart
Feeble and tired to the end of the road:
Look at me now, my face toward Balla,
Playing my music to empty pockets."

'The woman seemed to consider this. Then she nodded and lowered her sword and pushed open one of the gigantic doors with supernatural strength. And the poet and the Hound stepped inside.

"What do you see, Hound? Tell me what you see!" Raftery said, in a state of excitement.

"I see people. The place is crowded. Many of them are in strange garb. But there are other creatures too. From Faerie, I believe. I have no names for them. Many are horned. And many are winged. There are a couple of giants, standing with arms folded. This hall is so big, they don't have to stoop. Many people are drinking from horns. Everyone is watching a dais where stands a man in a brown robe with a golden girdle. He looks like a very powerful man. He has an aura about him. A kind of seriousness. A mystique. Standing before him is a tall, broad man in a strange, grey suit. His hair is tawny and tied at the back of his head with a piece of lace. I can't see his face. Nobody can, except for the man in the brown robe. I don't want to see his face."

"Why not?" Raftery asked.

"I'd be afraid it might be so beautiful there'd be something terrible in it."

'The bard nodded and said, "Continue."

"That's all there is really," Cù Chulainn said. "What do we do now?"

"We wait," the blind bard said.

"Who is that man, whose face I cannot see?" Cù Chulainn asked.

"He is known by many names. Most people call him Lucifer Morningstar. He is to be married."

"To whom?"

'A trumpet blast announced the arrival of the bride. The blast was so sudden and loud it almost knocked the Hound over.

"You're about to find out." Raftery said.

'The doors to the hall opened with a great, creaking noise. The audience fell silent almost immediately. The bride walked down the aisle. She was dressed in a traditional white wedding gown and veil, which seemed ethereal, almost ghostly to Cù Chulainn's eyes. She was accompanied by a dark-haired man in a blue suit, his shoulders broad. Again, Cù Chulainn didn't want to see this man's face. In fact, he didn't want to see any of their faces. He felt like they would be too bright to behold. When she reached the dais, she stepped up to the man waiting to become her husband.

"Who is she?" the Hound couldn't help but ask in an awed whisper.

"She is known by many names. I like Artemis, the virgin huntress," Raftery whispered back.

'Once the bride and groom stood before the man in the robe, he opened a book and began to read from it, in stentorian tones.

"Rintrah roars, and shakes his fires in the burden'd air,

Hungry clouds swag on the deep…"

"What was all that about?" the Hound asked, later on as they exited the hall. "That was the strangest wedding I've ever been to."

"The words were from an English poet and mystic, named William Blake. The Marriage of Heaven and Hell. Just like I told you."

"What does it all mean?"

"The union will produce a child who will bring peace to the world. Through imagination. That's what it's all about, Hound: imagination. I'm not talking about a new era or a new age. I'm talking about a new reality that will remain unchanged for as long as people walk the Earth. It's simple really. But you know how important ritual and formality are to people. You know how they like to complicate things."

"So, when does it happen?"

"Whenever people want it to happen."

'Cù Chulainn fell silent as they left the clearing, his mind brooding on all that had taken place.

'They returned to Emain Macha.

"Here we must part," Raftery said, when they had reached the river. Then, sensing that Cù Chulainn was troubled in his mind, he asked, "What ails you, Hound of Ulster?"

"Nothing has changed. I feel the same. Everything feels the same," Cù Chulainn said.

"You fear that it was all in vain," the bard said. "I don't think so. Remember you asked me why we were chosen to attend the wedding?"

"Yes."

"Well, the truth is I still don't know why we were, but the important thing is we made the journey. And, though it might not feel like it now, it has made its mark on you. On us. Does that make sense?"

"I guess so," Cù Chulainn said.

'And so, the Hound and the bard said their farewells and went on their separate ways. Cù Chulainn was no more troubled by dreams and visions of terrible warfare and the man on the cross. But sometimes he would dream of the wedding that had taken place and the faces, too bright to behold. And, though he was a little fearful, he knew that a great good had been done that day.'

Beard fell silent and when it became clear that he was finished, Summoner clapped his hands and said, 'Proper dancer, inne?'

'Yeah, that was really good,' I said.

Beard nodded but didn't say anything, just took a drag off his joint.

'I wish the others had heard it,' I said.

'Well, now that you have, you can tell them, can't you?' Summoner said. 'That's how it works.'

'I'd like to but I'm not much of a storyteller,' I said. 'Anyway, thanks Beard. I must return to my friends.'

Beard nodded and held up the joint he was smoking in a kind of salutation. I looked at Dan Lee and found he was watching me in a calm, intelligent way, puffing on his pipe. I had seen that look before. But I couldn't recall from whom. Anyway, I got up and returned to the others. They were in high spirits once more. Even Miranda and Sing had managed to shed the guilty look they had shared since leaving Shakespeare & Co. So, I went to the bar, determined not to cast gloom on everyone's good time. But it was hard. The anger had been replaced by shame. Although we weren't married, I felt like a cuckold and I couldn't help but feel foolish. So, I stood at the bar, drinking stout. I kept my eyes trained on an empty space on the far side of the bar. A patch of bare wall. I was afraid that if I looked around, I would see people laughing at me. I made an effort to dispel the paranoia by taking a look. My eye was immediately drawn to the two satyrs, sitting and smoking. They seemed to be looking directly at me and there was laughter in their eyes. Yes, behind the smoke they were smiling at me. Arrogantly. So, I returned my eyes to the bare patch of wall, defeated and dejected.

After a time, I felt a hand on my shoulder. I turned around and there was Dan Lee O'Brien, smiling at me. But it was a friendly kind of smile. I was surprised to see that he wasn't smoking. Dan lee without his pipe? It was unheard of. I tried to return the smile. 'Where's the pipe?' I asked.

'Resting in my pocket. I smoke too much,' the old man said.

'Yeah, me too.'

Nothing was said for a while and he continued to look at me, smiling. It was a sober kind of smile.

'So, what's the story with you?' Dan Lee asked.

'Ah, it's an old story. But, as I said, I'm not much of a storyteller.'

'Go on. Tell me. As briefly and concisely as you can.'

So, I did.

When I had finished, he said, 'I'm surprised at you, Steve. Most guys would give their right arm to have that in their life.'

'Yeah, I know. But…I guess I'm just a monogamous kind of guy.'

'But you're young. You should be out there experimenting. This is the 90s.'

'Yeah, I know. I know. It's just…'

'You feel guilty,' Dan Lee asked.

'Hell, no! Why should I feel guilty? I'm the one being cuckolded.'

'You are not being cuckolded. For one, you are not married. Two, this is not another man. And three, it sounds to me like you are being invited to be a part of it.'

'Yes, but where is the love?' I said.

'There seems to be enough love there to keep things going. You love Miranda, yes?'

'Yes.'

'And she loves you?'

'Yes. I think so.'

'And she and Sing love each other, yes?"

'Yes.'

'Well, there you go. There is enough love to keep you all happy. So, don't feel guilty.'

'I don't feel guilty.'

'So, why do you look like you have the weight of the world on your shoulders?' the old man said. 'Free your mind, Steve. You are too young to carry that weight.' Then he took hold of my arm and squeezed it gently. I nodded and looked at the patch of wall again. When I turned to look at him again, the old man was gone.

Free your mind. I thought about these words. Free love. Someone had talked to me about freedom not so long ago. Yes, it was the magician, Prospero. He had said real power consisted of setting a person free. I took another drink from my pint. The words went round and round in my head. Power. Freedom. Love. Guilt.

I felt another squeeze of my arm. I took my eyes off the patch of wall and turned to find Miranda looking up at me. Her eyes were half closed. She was clearly drunk again. But so was I. So, who cared? Who cared!

'I've been thinking,' I said.

'About what?' she said.

'About us,'

'And?'

'I think we can come to some kind of arrangement,' I said and smiled.

She kissed me, then. Longer and harder than she had ever kissed me. And it felt good. It felt right. When it had stopped, I looked over at the two smiling satyrs but this time they weren't smiling so much. Or so at least it appeared to me. Then she put her hands on my cheeks and turned my face back to her and kissed me some more.

That might very well have been the last time I drank in The Liberty. As I said, it was a building waiting to be condemned and it was, less than a year later. I have only good memories of the place. I think it is fair to say that there will never be another pub like it in Cork and when it was knocked down it was like the end of an era. Yes, as a Liminal it was the haunt of so many different creatures. In the darkness, nobody cared who you were, how you looked, where you came from. The students who visited it knew how to keep a secret. Yes, The Liberty was one of the best kept secrets of Cork's night life.

'Where to next?' I asked the others when myself and Miranda had returned to them.

'Hey, don't be in such a hurry. We just got here,' Ogma said.

'We've been here over an hour,' I said, after consulting my watch.

'Ah, really? You must remember time passes much quicker for me. Put away your timepiece, man. The night is young,' Ogma said.

'I just want to know the plan, is all,' I said.

'Ah, don't we all, Stevie?'

'Stop being so damn clever. You're worse than Summoner.'

'Nobody is worse than Summoner,' Ogma said and threw back his head and laughed. When he saw that I had nothing to say to this, he said, 'Next stop for you is Mac's. I'm going to stay here for a while though. I don't like nightclubs. Too noisy.'

Why Mac's?'

'Because it is owned by an IT deity. And the next step on your journey is the Information Age.'

'But Mac's is a naturals' nightclub,' I said.

'Yes, which is why Sing here is going to stay with me. We'll meet you by the fountain at about 2, ok?'

'Ok, if that's what you want,' I said. Then turning to James and Miranda, I said, 'looks like it's just us three again, guys.'

So, we left The Liberty. As it turned out, it wasn't just the three of us. Dan Lee came along as well. Have to say, there is something strange about him. Nothing sinister, mind you. It's just that he doesn't act like an old man a lot of the time. Sometimes there is something almost impish about him. And he never seems to get drunk. At least, I've never seen him drunk. He seems to like young people, though: there is nothing bitter or twisted about him. Altogether a nice man but, as I say, a little strange.

Once outside, the air hit us and with it the effects of the alcohol. James was hammered. I thought it might be hard to get him into Mac's but then I remembered that he was connected. He was our inside man. He worked for the God of IT. So, they'd have to leave him in, wouldn't they? All he had to say was that he was a tech support agent. But then I remembered that this was a naturals' nightclub. It was likely the doormen wouldn't give a shit what he did or who he worked for.

We walked down the South Main Street. Mac's was at the end of it, just across from the Beamish and Crawford Brewery. When the doormen saw the condition of James, they said to walk him around the block. We did so and when we returned, he had recovered enough to satisfy the bouncers. So, the four of us entered the nightclub.

Mac's was not my favourite nightclub. They played dance music, or 'rave' or 'trance' or whatever you want to call it, and I was more into grunge and metal: guitar-oriented music. To be perfectly honest, it left me a bit cold. It was completely computer generated. And the crowd left me a bit cold too, I have to say. Most of the people on the floor danced by themselves, as if on some private, inner journey or trip. It seemed like courtship went out the window. They just seemed so cold and remote. I remember what Ogma had said about us becoming a nation of introverts.

Like the doormen, the security inside all wore shades. They roamed about the place, looking for people to throw out. I went to the men's and puked up in one of the toilets. As always, this sobered me up quite a bit. I returned to my seat. James was there, drinking a Coke with ice. I sat down and looked about me. Dan Lee and Miranda were on the dance floor. He was shuffling back and forth and she was swinging her arms about, laughing. I had to laugh myself. Miranda was a terrible dancer and Dan Lee just didn't give a damn about what people thought of him. I had to admire him. But I also have to admit I was a little relieved to see that he wasn't smoking his pipe.

When I had stopped laughing, me and James managed a conversation. You know how it is, when you're in a nightclub and the music is so loud, you have to shout into the other person's ear. This means that irony and subtilty are often sacrificed. Add to this the alcohol factor and you end up with some very frank and direct conversations.

'What's so funny?' James asked

'It's Miranda. She's a terrible dancer.'

'Better than you, I'd bet.'

'Yeah, you're right. Have to say, though. I don't know how people can dance to this music. It has no sex in it.'

'You mean you don't find that driving, pumping beat sexy?'

'Not at all. It leaves me cold. Everything about this place leaves me cold. Tell me, is this really the future, James?'

'It is like a ghost of the future, yes. Does it scare you?'

'Yes, it does. Kind of.'

'Yeah, I know. A lot of people feel that way. They are fearful of this new technology. Where will it will take us.'

'You're an IT guy, James. Where do you think it will take us?'

'Well, in a nutshell, we are all going to become closer but at the same time we are going to become further apart. It's that second one that we have to be careful about.'

'I see. You're a smart guy, James. Did I ever tell you that?'

'Not as smart as him,' he said, pointing his finger at a young man who sat alone nearby. Like the bouncers, he wore shades but, instead of a t-shirt, he had a business suit on. His hair was a reddish-brown crewcut. He had a laptop computer on his thighs and he was busy typing on it. Beside him, on a small table, was a creamy pint of stout.

'Who's he when he's at home?' I asked.

'That's Mac. The owner,' James said.

'Doesn't look very godlike to me. You think he'd talk to me?'

'Only one way to find out.'

'James, if I get kicked out, I'm going to be royally pissed at you.'

'I thought you didn't like the place?'

'Yes, but I like the prospect of a boot print on my ass less,' I said.

'I can introduce you, if you want.'

'You know him?'

'Well…yes. He doesn't know me but I know him. If you get my drift,' James said.

'I don't know. I'm a little intimidated.'

'Don't worry. He's a nice fellow. Think of all the young people he has been nice to in this country. He's no villain. Unless you call being rich a crime.'

'Ok. Let's do it.'

So, we got up off the seat and approached the god. James staggered a bit but aside from that it was a good approach. The god was just taking a sip from his pint when he saw us coming. James offered his hand and the deity accepted it and shook it. They had what looked to be a short but animated conversation before James introduced me.

'Hi, Steve. Nice to meet you,' the god said in a pure, polite North-side accent.

'Uh, hi Mac. Is it ok if I call you Mac?'

'I've been called worse things, ha ha. Course it is. What can I do for you, Steve?'

'Uh, I just wanted to ask a few questions. I won't be long.'

'Shoot, buddy.'

'Well, first of all, are you a Norrie? Because you sure as Hell sound like one.'

Mac laughed at this before saying, 'Yes, I'm a Norrie. Sure, don't I have my headquarters there? Up near Knocknaheeney?'

'Yes, but there aren't many North-siders who work there,' I couldn't help pointing out.

'Yes, but things will change, in time, hopefully.'

'Yeah. Let's hope so. Uh, look, so what I really wanted to ask you is…a friend of mine. Ogma is his name. He said that you were trying to turn us all into introverts. A nation of introverts. Is that true?'

'That is not my plan,' Mac said.

'But it might happen.'

'If it does, it won't be at my instigation.'

'That won't be much comfort,' I said.

'Look, Steven. I'm a god but I can't predict the future, let alone control it. But as long as there are people like you and Ogma out there to warn us of the potential dangers, then I think we are going to be alright.'

'So, you accept that it is a danger?'

'Yes. You've told me and I agree it is a concern. I'll see what I can do about it. Thanks for enlightening me.'

'Hey, that's really neat. Thanks for listening. It's really Ogma you should be thanking, though.'

'Have you any other questions?'

'Um, yes. What are you doing here with the computer? Don't you know you shouldn't mix business with pleasure?' I said and grinned.

The god looked at the computer, then at the pint on his table.

'You know something, Steve? You're absolutely right,' he said and then shut the laptop and put it aside.

'Now, you're getting it!' I said. 'Come join us, why don't you?'

'Don't mind if I do,' Mac said and picked up his pint.

I returned to James with Mac following me. We sat down and watched the dancers. Miranda and Dan Lee were still fooling about on the floor.

'Nice guy,' I said to James.

'I told you so,' he replied. 'What did you talk about?'

'Just the future. You know, I actually think we are going to be ok.'

'I agree,' James said and sipped from his Coke.

I took out my cigarettes and offered one to Mac. He seemed indecisive. 'Go on, take one!' I said. And so, he did. When we had lit up, I said to him, 'Can I ask you a personal question?'

'Yeah, go ahead.'

'Why the shades?'

Mac smiled and said, 'Do you really want to know?'

'Sure.'

So, he took off the shades and turned to look at me directly. His eyes were blank. Like an ancient Greek statue. 'Does that answer your question?' he said.

'Ah I see. You're not blind, are you?' I asked.

'No. I can see just fine. It's just that people find it a bit disturbing. So, I wear the shades.'

'And what about the bouncers?'

'No, they are all normal. The sun glasses are just part of the uniform. Not my idea, by the way.' He put on the shades again.

'What about this music?'

'Also, not my idea. I'm an 80s man myself. Give me some A-ha and Police any day of the week.'

'You know, Mac, for the owner of this place you don't seem to have much of a say in the running of it,' I said.

'I do. But I like to keep it a fairly laidback operation,' Mac said, and took a deep sip from his pint.

'Well, then there's hope for us yet,' I said.

At this point, Dan Lee and Miranda left the dance floor and walked over to where we were seated. Dan Lee sat down, a little exhausted but Miranda grabbed my hand and pulled me up, with the intention of dragging me onto the dance floor.

'Excuse me!' I said to Mac and then I was dancing, or attempting to dance, on the floor.

Like Miranda, I swung my arms about and moved my head from side to side. And, I have to admit, I still had my trench coat on. But what the Hell? Miranda didn't seem to mind. Looking back on it, I do cringe a bit. But only a little. Of course, it was too loud for conversation. So, we just danced and grinned at each other. It reminded me of earlier days. Before I met Miranda. When dancing with a girl was the first step toward scoring with her. And I didn't give a shit about how stupid I looked. After a while, I enclosed her in my coat and kissed her deeply. She grabbed my bum and squeezed it. Then we returned to the seats and had the best snog I had had in a long time.

Later on, we met Ogma and Sing at the fountain in the city centre, as planned. Sing and Miranda sat on the parapet, deep in conversation again. Sing was wrapped up in what appeared to be John Summoner's trench coat and had a woolly hat on her head, to hide her hair. There was no sign of Summoner. Ogma and James were standing nearby, chatting with a bunch of students. I was talking to the god, Dionysus, who also sat on the parapet of the fountain. He seemed to have sobered up completely. He wore a black leather jacket and baggy, blue jeans.

'So, Stevie,' he asked, 'Did you find any drama on your pub crawl, today?'

'Yes, a bit.'

'And how did it turn out? A tragedy? Or a comedy?'

'A comedy,' I said. 'Definitely a comedy.'

'Good,' the god said and smiled.

'How was your day?' I asked him.

'Oh, not much happened. I was obliterated. Then I sobered up and now I'm here.'

'We've met here before, a few times. Why do you like it here?'

'Isn't it obvious? I come here for the drama.' The god nodded in the direction of a gang of girls who were, apparently, being shepherded by a couple of guys. An argument broke out between two of the girls. It was loud and high pitched and not very lovely at all.

'Hang about. We might have a fight,' the god said.

'I don't like fights. I get nervous,' I said.

'What's there to be nervous about? You are only a spectator.'

'Wouldn't you prefer a bit of peace?'

'Peace? Peace? Nothing ever came of peace, Stevie. Nothing,' the god said.

'What do you mean? Don't you like to read? Or have a nice, civilised conversation?'

'It's because of war that you can enjoy those luxuries.'

I tried to think up an answer, but my wits were clouded by alcohol. 'Ah, this isn't fair! I'm drunk and you're sober!' I said, at last.

Dionysus laughed and said, 'Yes, I know. Funny how things turn out, isn't it?'

There was a loud splash, and a general cheer broke out. I looked across the way. A girl had been dropped into the fountain and was now standing, knee deep in water, her dress clinging to her thighs and breasts. She was making a noise that sounded like part laugh and part scream.

'Someone's enjoying themselves,' the god said.

'You're a cool customer, aren't you?' I said to him.

'No, I'm just a spectator. Like you are,' the god said. 'All alone. Watching. In the darkness.'

'You don't seem to think it's much fun.'

'I prefer the ancient way. When there wasn't that much distance separating actor and spectator.'

'I think we've had this conversation before,' I said.

'Have we? I'm sorry. I repeat myself. Don't you know I'm basically a fertility god? Renewal is what I'm all about,' the god said and grinned.

'Oh, not you as well,' I complained.

'Not me as well what?'

'Everyone seems to think they are a clever clog, except me.'

'Ah, Stevie. The Greeks were such a clever people.'

'Where is your brother, Apollo?'

'I don't know. Probably tucked up in bed with a good book.'

'You're very different.'

'Don't I know it. It's something he's never forgiven me for. Being different.'

'Is that why you drink so much?' I asked.

'Partly, I guess. It's also out of a sense of duty. But most of all, it is out of boredom.'

'I notice you are not drinking now.'

'That's right. But I would if I had any.'

'What are you saying, I'm boring?'

'Listen Stevie. I've been on this planet for over 2,500 years. You try staying interested in people after that amount of time. Believe me, it's not easy.'

'Ok, let me see if I can get you a drink,' I said. 'Hey, Ogma!'

The god turned around from the students he was regaling.

'This man is thirsty. Got any drink on you?' I said.

Ogma walked over, pulling a naggin out of his trouser pocket as he did so. He tossed it at us and Dionysus caught it. It was a naggin of Jack Daniels. The wine god thanked him and Ogma returned to his audience.

'He doesn't seem bored. And he's been here as long as you have,' I said to the god.

'That's because he is trying to score, Stevie. Your dick never loses interest until it gets what it wants. Understand?'

I laughed and nodded. 'Here, let me have some of that.' The god handed me the naggin and I sipped from it. 'So, what's your story? Is there a Mrs Dionysus?'

'No, I never married. Came close a couple of times but…'

'But what?'

'I think I understand them too well. To marry one of them, I mean.'

'Explain,' I said.

'Well, men like to figure things out, right? And when they've figured one thing out, they'll move on to another. So, that's why women like to keep them guessing. Keep them interested. The truth is women are exactly the same as us. They think exactly like we do.'

'And that turns you off them?'

'It turns me off marrying one of them, yes. But I still like a good shag every now and then.'

'You know, if you weren't a god, I'd feel sorry for you,' I said.

'I'm sorry too,' he said and sighed. He took a sip of Jack Daniels. 'So, what about you? You married? Girlfriend?'

'I have a girlfriend,' I said and looked over at Miranda, to make sure she wasn't listening in. 'She's a Lesbian,' I said, quietly.

'You mean bi-sexual. If you're still in a relationship with her, that means she's bisexual.'

'Ok, bisexual then. If you're such an expert, maybe you could give me some advice.'

'About what?'

'I've never been in bed with two women before. I mean, what do I do? Where do I start?'

'Ah, Stevie. You'll work it out,' the god said and smiled before taking another sip. 'Yes, you'll work it out.'

'That's it? That's all you have to say?'

Dionysus sighed again, before saying, 'Think of it as a drama. With three players. And instead of talking through verbal language you are talking with your bodies. Your wants and needs. Your consents. Your limits. It's almost like a negotiation. Ah, you are such a lucky boy, Stevie.'

I thought about what he had said for a half a minute before coming up with this: 'Ok, if sex is a drama, is it a comedy or a tragedy?'

'I would have thought that was obvious. For the man, it is a tragedy and for the woman, it is a comedy.'

'Explain.'

'Well, the man loses his mojo, doesn't he? That's a tragedy. But the woman gains love. Which means for her it is a comedy. Yes, the bedroom is very much a place where women rule.'

As it turned out, there was no need for trepidation. Sing slept on the leather couch in the living room of our apartment, leaving the bedroom to just me and Miranda.

We made love.

There was a frantic urgency to Miranda's love making which she had never shown before. I felt like I was being rewarded. Maybe for accepting Sing into our lives. We were no longer a couple but a triple, and I think Miranda wanted to show me that she loved me all the more for it. Miranda liked to be on top and as she rode me, she lowered her head and whispered in my ear profanities mixed with sweet words. Some words were even in a language I didn't understand. It was almost like she was casting a spell. A spell to improve our love life. And it worked!

Even though I was far gone into drink, it was one of the best bouts of sex that I have ever experienced. I found myself wondering if Sing had maybe taught her some of those words. I remembered how they always seemed to be deep into a private conversation. I found myself wondering if this was a taste of things to come. If so, then yes, I was a lucky boy indeed. I remembered what Dionysus had said about sex being a tragedy for men. I could see where he was coming from, but that night I didn't feel any pain at all. The only thing I was at a loss for was words.

When I sleep drunk, I always have very vivid dreams, or nightmares, and they always have the same theme: finding my way home. I cross fields and hills. Enter and exit strange bars, hotels and houses. I try to catch buses in towns that don't even exist. Yes, through wildernesses urban and rural, I ceaselessly quest for home. Doesn't sound very nightmarish, does it? But if you think about it, being homeless is probably one of the worst things that could conceivably happen to a person. And in these dreams, I am always alone.

But that night, I dreamt that I finally got home. Not to our apartment near the North Cathedral. But to my old house in Knocknaheeney. No. 29, Killiney Heights. I was in the living room, seated in an armchair. There were three others: my father was seated in his armchair, by the fire. He had died two years previously from a heart attack, while still a very young man. In the couch across from him were John Summoner and Jim Morrison. Summoner was without his trench coat, which was unheard of. Then, I remembered Sing wrapped in it earlier by the fountain. This made me realise that it wasn't just a dream but another psychic episode.

'Hey,' I said to no-one in particular.

'Hey, mate,' Summoner said. 'Your father was good enough to allow us in here. To talk. Thanks again, Mr. J.'

'No worries,' my father said.

'These are my friends, Dad,' I said.

'Yes, I know, Steve.'

'Ok. So, what do you want to talk about?' I asked.

'Well, now that you've finished your epic pub crawl, we thought you might have some questions,' Summoner said.

I thought about it before saying, 'There are a couple of things I'm wondering about. That maybe you could throw light on.'

'Shoot, Stevie.'

'Well, first of all, where were the villains? I mean, we go on a pub crawl through the history of Western Civilisation and there are no villains. Surely there must be at least one?'

'Well, maybe there isn't. Maybe in a truly civilised society there are no villains, only victims. Do you understand?' Summoner said.

'Do you really believe that?' I asked.

'I don't know, Steve. I think it's worth thinking about, though. Don't you?'

'I guess so.'

There was a moment of pensive silence.

'Ok, what else is on your mind?' Summoner asked.

'Well, I'm wondering was it all destiny or was it just us? Was everything plotted before we set out, or did we plot it ourselves? Do you get me?'

'Yes. I think Jim might have something to say on this.'

'Hey, Steve,' Jim said. 'I think the answer to your question is that both destiny and freewill were involved. I'm no authority but…I've thought about this question a lot over the years and I've come to believe that…there is freedom within fate. Think of yourself as being in a dance with destiny…An intimate dance that lasts your entire lifetime…Sometimes you lead and sometimes you are led. Does that make sense?'

'Hmmm. Ok,' I said.

'Is there anything else?' Summoner asked.

'Dad, what are you doing here?' I said to my old man.

'I'm just making sure these two don't corrupt you, Steve,' he replied.

'Come on, Mr. J. We're here to help him. The lad wants to be a magician,' Summoner said.

'Yes, I know that. I just don't want him meddling in the dark arts.'

'Neither do we.'

'I know your reputation, John Summoner. It is not a good one. And you, Morrison,' he said. 'You've corrupted too many youths.'

'You shouldn't believe everything you read, Mr. Jones. Or see, for that matter,' Morrison said.

'What's that supposed to mean?'

'He's talking about the biographers and that bloody film by Oliver Stone. It's they who are responsible for corrupting the youths,' Summoner said. 'But let's ask Steve himself. Do you feel like we are trying to corrupt you?'

'No. Maybe confuse me at times. But not corrupt me.'

My father sighed and said, 'I just don't want you making the same mistakes I did, Steve.'

'What do you mean? You never practiced magic, Dad.'

'No, you're wrong, son. I was into it when I was your age. Heavily into it. I had my heroes. I had my dreams. But I had my demons too. And those demons got the better of me.'

'What happened, Dad?'

'It's complicated, son. Hopefully you will never know.'

'I want to know.'

'Don't say that, Steve. Trust me. You don't.'

There was a silence before he continued, 'Now, listen here, John Summoner. I know your reputation but I also know that you're an Englishman, and the English people are good people. I've learned that through experience. So, I'm not going to judge you. I'm going to give you a chance. But if I hear the slightest bit of rumour that you are putting badness into the heart of my son, I will wipe you out. The same goes for you, Morrison.'

'Dad, they're trying to help me get to where I want to be,' I said.

'It's ok, Steve. I'm sure they'll understand if I'm being protective.'

'Mr. J, we totally understand,' Summoner said. 'Steve's on the right road and we intend to keep him on it.'

'Ok. We're all agreed so. We understand each other,' my father said. 'So, I'll be seeing you again, son.'

'Don't go, Dad.'

'I have to Steve,' he said and got up. He looked at me through steady blue eyes and rubbed his hands together as he so often did. 'Don't worry, I'll check in on you from time to time.'

'I want to talk, Dad.'

'Oh, there'll be plenty of time for that, when the time comes around,' he said.

'Don't go.'

'Be careful, Steve,' he said and vanished. So, did Summoner and Morrison. I was left alone in the room with nothing but tears for company.

III

Remember when I said that hangovers weren't a problem for me? Well, they weren't. Not until that morning after the crawl, that is. It was the first real hangover I reckon I've ever had. And it was bad, man. I mean, it was a vicious bastard.

I woke up alone. The song, Break on Through, by The Doors was playing in the living room. I could smell a fry coming from the kitchen. My head felt like someone had deposited a bowling ball in it.

I groaned and lay there, suffering. Looking at the ceiling. Smelling the fry. Feeling sick. I just wanted to go back to sleep. Back to my little bunker and let the bombs explode somewhere above me. Like distant thunder. Harmless. Until it was safe to emerge.

But sleep was denied to me. Miranda popped her head around the door and said, 'Get up, Steve. Breakfast's ready.'

Now, I had two courses open to me: I could either go back to sleep and risk the wrath of Miranda. Or I could get up and take breakfast, at the risk of throwing up, which would also upset Miranda. I reckoned the second option was the safest course to take. After I had gotten up and dressed, maybe the hangover would have dissipated a little. And if it didn't, at least she'd know that I tried.

So, I got up and dressed slowly. Like a man doing it for the first time. I groaned again. I could hear the music of the Doors coming from next door:

When I had dressed, I paid a visit to the toilet. I looked in the mirror and the face I saw looking back at me was like a reject of Dionysus. My eyes were bloodshot and my mouth was heavy and stained by tobacco. My hair was a mess. I groaned again.

Then I relieved myself in the toilet bowl. I do believe it was the longest lasting urination I have ever had. It kept going and going and going. It just wouldn't stop. When it finally did, I felt a little better. But not much. I washed my hands and then I splashed cold water on my face. It seemed like the natural thing to do. But it didn't make much of a difference, either to the way I looked or felt.

I shuffled out of the toilet. As I passed the bedroom, I was tempted to go back to bed. It would be warm and safe and blissful there. But I thought again of Miranda. I really didn't want to upset her, so I walked toward the living room and opened the door. Ready to face the music.

James was in the armchair. He looked like he was suffering as much as I was. He had the same shell-shocked look about him. This did make me feel a little better. His skin was pale, his mouth drawn and his eyes looked into the middle distance. When I entered, he looked up at me and attempted a smile and a nod. He got about halfway there.

'How's the head?' I asked.

'Wrecked,' he said.

Sing was curled up on the far side of the sofa, holding a mug of coffee with both hands. I expected her to smile at my condition. You know the one. The smile the blessed have for the damned? But she didn't. She smiled at me but it was a small, enigmatic one. So, that was two out of three in my favour. I sat down on the other side of the couch and waited for Miranda. It had been a great night and I had no reason to fear her. I could remember everything and I was sure she did too. But I have to admit to a feeling of relief when she came in and put my afternoon breakfast fry up on the table before me: her eyes were also bloodshot and her hands tremored a little.

'Thanks, babe,' I mumbled.

The food before me was a classic Irish heart attack on a plate. Sausages, rashers, eggs, a cloven tomato and mushrooms. All fried. I looked at it and knew straight away that I was defeated. I would never be able to eat this. As I studied it, Miranda returned from the kitchen and put a mug of coffee beside the plate. I looked up at her and mumbled another thanks. She sat down opposite me, on a chair she had taken from the kitchen. She lit up a cigarette and sat there, smoking, just looking at me. I was reminded of her when we first got together. That calm, perceptive, 'female student gaze' that she used to have.

I managed a sausage and a couple of mushrooms before I put down my fork and knife, in defeat. 'I'm sorry, babe,' I said.

She sighed and rolled her eyes before getting up and taking the plate and returning to the kitchen with it. I listened for banging noises but there were none. That meant she wasn't too pissed off about it. I sighed in relief and took a sip of coffee.

'What time is it?' I asked no-one in particular.

'Just after 2:30.' James said.

'What a night, eh?' I said. 'What a day and night.'

James managed a smile and said, 'we're paying for it now, though.'

'Aren't we just.'

Miranda returned and sat down again, smoking.

'How do you feel?' I asked her.

'A bit delicate but I'll survive,' she said.

I sat back and let out a mixture of a sigh and a groan, searching my pockets for cigarettes.

'Here,' Miranda said and tossed a packet over to me.

I took one out and lit up. I regretted it instantly as it made me feel sick again. I smoked it about half way before giving up and crushing it out on the ashtray.

The music of The Doors continued to play from the stereo. It wasn't what you would call blasting but to my ears it was way too loud.

'Could we turn that off?' I asked no-one in particular. Miranda got up and did so. 'Sorry, Jim,' I said.

I thought of telling them about my visitation during the night but elected not to. The truth was, I was sick of the psychic and the supernatural and I guessed they were too. It occurred to me that maybe I was paying the price for that as well as the drink. That socialising with gods had its cost. Whatever the case, I just wanted a day free from magic. Which is why, when James said we should go for a cure, I insisted that it be a natural's pub. He suggested The Far Side which was next door to Mac's. I agreed heartily. We asked the girls if they wanted to come along. Sing shook her head, a little look of disgust on her face. Miranda also shook her head, but her face didn't register anything.

When we got outside, my system continued to recover. I thought that I mightn't even need a cure after all but when I looked at James, I could see that he plainly did. But even so, the truth was we were in new territory as far as abusing alcohol went and I wanted to find out if 'hair of the dog' really did work.

The Far Side was an unusual pub. It was made up of heavily plastered corridors and spaces and windows, the overall effect being almost like a mine, as if a gang of dwarves had went to work on it for a few months. When we entered and approached the bar, I was pleased to see Billy, my old friend from the band, propping up the bar on his own. We exchanged words, ordered our pints and when they had been served, we asked Billy if he wanted to join us at a table. This was out of a genuine love for the guy, but it also gave me an excuse not to talk about the 'business'.

'What's the story?' Billy said after we had settled down. He was a South-sider and so the expression didn't sound quite right out of his mouth but no-one's perfect, right?

'We're recovering. From a pub crawl we went on yesterday,' I said. 'James here suggested hair of the dog.'

'Ah, the old reliable. Where did ye go?'

'All over the place,' I said. 'We ended up in Mac's. It was a legendary day, I can tell you that much. How about yourself? Were you out last night?'

'No, I was just in town today and I felt hot and thirsty so I came in here to cool down with a pint.'

'Fair play to ya,' I said.

'You still in the magic game?'

'Magic? A little bit. It's a fool's game really, though. You still playing music?'

'I'm not in a band but I still play. When I have the time.'

'You still an IT guy?'

'Yep.'

'So is James,' I said. James managed a queasy smile.

'Jesus, you look terrible, James,' Billy said. 'Get that pint down you and we'll order you another one.'

'So, we were talking about the coming revolution last night,' I said.

'What's that?' Billy said.

'The information revolution?'

'Oh, that.'

'You don't sound too excited about it,' I said.

'Well when you work nine to five, five days a week, in front of a computer screen, it gets hard to be excited about it. Don't get me wrong. Change is coming. Big change. But I think people will run the risk of becoming too reliant on the technology.'

'You think so?' I asked.

'Yes.'

We sipped our pints in silence. I was feeling much better but James still had a way to go.

'It's like that movie, *Terminator*. You know, where the machines take over the planet? I think we will run the risk of becoming slaves to the technology,' Billy said.

'Hmmm. Wise words,' I said.

Another silence fell on us. I had a nice mellow buzz going. Until Billy asked me about Miranda. Which put me I mind of Sing. Which troubled me.

'Yeah, she's fine. What about you? How's the love life?'

'Between girlfriends at the moment.'

I was tempted to say *me too* but I decided not to.

'I don't know is it worth it?' James piped up. We looked at him.

'Is what worth it?' Billy repeated.

'Girlfriends.'

'Why do you say that?' I asked him.

'Well, you spend so much time and energy trying to win one and once you do, well is it really worth it? I mean, have you ever felt like "What am I doing here?".'

'Yeah, I suppose that's true,' Billy said.

I nodded in acquiescence. 'Don't get me wrong. I love my girlfriend to bits. But I do feel that way sometimes.'

'Someone should write a song about it,' Billy said and laughed. 'No, but seriously, where would we be without them?"

We shared another pensive silence. It was broken by the sound of breaking glass. Somewhere near the bar. We looked in that direction, but we were unable to see what had happened as it was out of our line of sight. We looked at each other, with raised eyebrows. Then there was the sound of another glass breaking and it was followed by a curse. I got up and the others did too. When I had turned the corner and the bar was in view, I could see the barman vaulting over the counter and a couple of patrons standing away from it. Another glass was broken, followed by the smashing of a mirror that was on the far side of the bar. The barman cursed again. I also cursed inwardly but for a different reason: gone was my hope of having a day free of the psychic and the supernatural. It was plainly a poltergeist.

'Ok, leave it to me,' I said to the barman and the customers. If I'd had a badge I would have flashed it at them, briefly, wearily. I stood at the bar. An ashtray was picked up by the spirit and the contents were thrown at me. Ash and fag butts rained down on my face.

I stayed calm. 'Ok, that's enough of that. Show yourself,' I said.

A bar stool on the other side of the bar was pushed over. A pint glass, half filled with stout, was raised. I guessed the spirit's intentions.

'Go on. I dare you. I dare you,' I said. The spirit hesitated and then put down the glass. 'Good,' I said. 'Now, are you going to show yourself and maybe we can talk about this?' I said to the spirit. Nothing happened. 'I think you'll have guessed by now that I'm not afraid of you,' I said. 'So, show yourself and let's talk.'

It was a young woman, about my age. Mid-twenties that is. She was clad in a short, figure-hugging dress. Her hair was peroxide blonde and she was dolled up, but tastefully so. The overall impression she made was that of a young woman ready to go nightclubbing. 'That's better,' I said.

'How do I get out of here?' she asked. Turning around. I looked at the barman. He went around the corner of the bar and opened a door for her.

She walked towards me, holding a slim handbag. Her shoulders were tensed up and she looked on the verge of tears. We sat down in a corner, as far away from the others as possible.

'I'm Steve,' I said.

'Iris,' she said.

'Nice name.'

'Thanks.'

'So, Iris, are you going to tell me what this is about?'

She looked at me with a slightly fierce expression.

'When did you die?' I asked her.

For a moment she looked about ready to bite my head off, but she didn't. Instead she broke down into tears. 'Why do you care?' she asked.

'I just want to know how long you've been suffering and why?'

'It was a car crash, ok? A couple of months ago. Now, are you happy?'

'No,' I said.

'Why not?'

'Because I want to know your story and I don't think you'll be able to rest until you tell someone.'

She seemed to recover, taking a handkerchief out of her bag before applying it to her eyes. 'You want to know my story?'

'Yes.'

'I just want to know why the fuck I have to go, ok? I don't want to leave. I don't want to leave this place. I don't want to leave this decade. Why does the party have to end? Why?'

'It's ok to feel that way,' I said. 'We all do. Living or dead. But who knows what party awaits us once we cross over?'

'Oh, that is so lame,' she said, sniffling.

'Yeah, I know,' I said. 'I didn't know what else to say.'

'That is so fucking lame,' she said and started to laugh. I joined her.

'Tell me your story, Iris,' I said after the laughing spell had passed.

'You think it will ease my passing?'

'Yes. But I also just want to hear it. For myself.'

'God, I could do with a drink and a smoke,' she said.

'Sorry but I can't help you with that.'

'Yeah, I know. I'm just saying.'

'Unless I drink and smoke for the two of us?' I said. She nodded and smiled. When she smiled I caught a hint of how beautiful she must have been. It was a roguish smile but in a feminine way. I picked up my glass and emptied most of the contents. Then I liberated two cigarettes, put them in my mouth and lit them. She laughed.

'So, Iris. What is your story?' I said at last.

'You really want to know, Steve?'

'Yes, I really want to know.

'Ok. Well. There isn't that much to tell. But when I think about it, I suppose it really only started when I left secondary school. You see, I left my family at the same time. My father was a religious nut. He tried to control almost every aspect of my life. I sometimes wonder what the hell he was thinking because if there is one way to drive your kids away from you it's by trying to impose your god damned religion on every aspect of their lives.

I wonder was he doing it deliberately to make me independent? Or did he just think it was the only way to bring up a kid? School sucked as well. I hated it. Couldn't wait to be free of it.

'So, I left school and left my father at the same time. I got a job as a waitress and I made a friend named Julia. We ended up sharing an apartment. Julia introduced me to the twin joys of alcohol and cigarettes, amongst other things. Looking back on it, those were probably the best days of my life. I mean, I know it doesn't sound like much. I guess I'm just easy to please. Give me some music, drink and a good conversation and that's all I need. When I think about those years, I remember the laughter more than anything else. Julia was really funny. She should have been a stand-up comedian. I really gained character and confidence in that first flowering of freedom and independence. My time in school and at my family home seemed like a previous existence. I changed so much and I exulted in that change. I left the past far, far behind me.

'The next thing I discovered was nightclubs. And with nightclubs came sex and drugs. If we wanted to score with guys, we went to Gorby's nightclub, off Oliver Plunkett street. If we just wanted to dance, we would go to Mac's. When I say drugs, what I really mean is Ecstasy. This drug is more suited to the dance scene at Mac's than the indie rock vibe at Gorby's. Me, I preferred to rave than to rock, so I took a lot of E. Everyone was taking it back then. But it was at Gorby's that I met the love of my life. Frank was his name. He was the sweetest, most gentle-hearted guy you could ever meet. We fell in love fast. I was also in college around this time, studying software engineering. I did well. Discovered brains I never knew I had. On leaving college, I was lucky enough to get a job as a software tester in Cork. I didn't even have to move!

'So, there I was. My confidence and self-esteem at a record high. Earning good money. And very much in love. And still very young. One of my best memories from that time was when me and Frank went camping one Summer's night at the Lee fields. It was just the two of us. Frank brought along a fishing rod. He wanted to fish but all he caught were eels. He was no fisherman. We made love right there by the river. I remember looking over his shoulder, up at the stars, and thinking life just doesn't get any better than this.

'But don't get me wrong. There were dark days too. One of my friends committed suicide. He was a quiet lad from the country. I met him through Frank. Why did he do it? We don't know. He didn't leave a note. Sometimes when I think of him, I get mad. Kind of like the way I feel about Kurt Cobain. But mostly I just miss him and ask why, Oh why, oh why didn't you leave a note? Not long after that I developed an unhealthy Ecstasy habit. I was taking way too much of the stuff. I would drop five or six pills in one night. I think it might partly have been related to my friend's suicide but mainly it was because it just made me feel so damned good. Where was Frank during all this? Well, he suffered too. And he got high as much as I did. We really were quite a couple. And how did it all end? Well, with a bang, you might say. A car crash. In the countryside. With some mad bitch I didn't even know the name of at the wheel. I was very drunk and so was she. We hit a stone wall. Death on impact. Say good night, Iris. Say good night.'

'That's quite a story,' I said, when it was clear that she had finished.

'Thanks.'

'No, I mean, really. It sounds like you've done a lot of living.'

'You really think so? I think I've done hardly any at all. That's why I feel cheated,' she said.

'Your story. It's the story of the 90s. Can't you see that?'

'Is it? I just don't want it to end. Why does it have to end?'

'It doesn't end. You're just moving on. To the great gig in the sky, as they say.'

'Do you really believe that?' she asked.

'Yes, I do.'

'I think I'd prefer to stay here. Talking with you.'

'I'm flattered that you would say that, Iris,' I said. 'But there aren't many people like me around. It's best to move on.'

There was a hint of her previous temper flaring up.

'Hey. You can't hang around spending all your time breaking up bars, Iris,' I said.

'I can try.'

'What's the point?'

'There isn't one. It just feels good. You know, like the Ecstasy.'

'And what about the people you are terrifying? Do you think they deserve it?'

'Yes,' she said.

'Why?'

'Because they are smug.'

'Ah, I see. So, you are on a ghostly crusade against smugness.'

'Yes. I am.'

I nodded my head in a resigned kind of way. She started to laugh. So did I. Pretty soon we were in bits. And, inevitably, the laughter turned to tears.

'So, I really have to go?' she said.

I nodded.

'Ok. Do you really think I've done a lot of living?'

'More than most,' I said.

She nodded and wiped her face with her handkerchief. 'Thanks, Steve,' she said and was gone.

I returned to the others. As I did so, I signalled to the barman that everything was ok again. For him, that is. For myself, I did not feel ok. Having to talk down ghosts is always a depressing business as it is a reminder of my mortality. And, on this day, I really was hoping that I would be free from the business. For just one day.

'What was that all about?' Billy asked. He looked a bit awestruck.

'Just another ghost needing to tell their story,' I said.

'Does this have something to do with the magic?'

'It has everything to do with the magic.'

'Jeez, I didn't realise you were in so deep,' Billy said.

'Poltergeist?' James asked. He was looking much better. Seemed like the hair of the dog was working.

'Yes. I'll tell you about her later,' I said.

'Must take balls to do something like that. Confront a ghost,' Billy said.

'Not really. When you do it as often as I do, it loses the fear factor.'

'Still, you could have been injured by one of those glasses flying about.'

'That's true. Just an occupational hazard, I guess.'

'So, what, did you just send her on her way?' Billy said.

'In a manner of speaking.'

'To where? Heaven?'

'To the great gig in the sky,' I said. At this point I was getting a little sick of Billy's questioning. So, I said, 'I'm done here. If you guys want to carry on drinking without me, I won't be offended. I'm going back to the apartment.'

'You sure, Steve?' James asked.

'I'm sure.'

'Gee, sorry for pestering you, Steve,' Billy said.

'No, you didn't. I'm just feeling a bit…like I need to get back to the apartment. You guys take it easy,' I said as I put on my trench coat.

'Yeah, you too,' James said.

'Yeah, take care,' Billy said.

And I was gone.

It was good to be out in the fresh air again. My hangover had completely cleared and the incident with the ghost was rapidly receding in my mind. Except for one thing. The question of whether or not she had lived a full life stayed with me. I asked myself this same question. Had I led a full life thus far? I had certainly led an interesting life. That was for sure. I had chosen a path less taken. Was it full? How can you tell? How can anyone tell? I suppose the best anyone can do is to try to enjoy life as best they can but expect to suffer. Yes, it was the same for all of us.

That afternoon as I walked up Shandon Street in the warm sunlight, I felt a species of joy that I had never felt before. A kind of civilised joy. It was the closest I've ever come to a truly philanthropic state of heart and mind. And it occurred to me that maybe that was the fullest life anyone could lead. A life of Universal love, tolerance and sympathetic joy. Because these were the hardest things to feel. And the best things in life do not come easy.

So, I arrived at our apartment with these lofty thoughts in my head. I strolled about the place looking for the girls until I found them in our bedroom. They were in our bed. Just lying there, supine, under the covers. When Miranda saw me she gave me a little smile and wave of her hand. Sing remained quiet, as always. She had the blanket pulled up over her breasts. I grinned at them and walked toward the bed.

'Make some room for me,' I said and climbed in between them, putting my arms around their shoulders. We stayed that way for a while, in silence. Birdsong came from outside the window. I felt an intense delight.

Miranda asked, 'Did you get your cure?'

'We did. And I had a conversation with a ghost.'

'What about?'

'I helped her to move on.'

'Is that why you are in such good spirits?' Miranda asked.

'Maybe. I guess I'm just feeling a kind of philanthropic joy. It's a rare feeling. I'm just enjoying it while it lasts.'

I started to hum. A kind of happy, tuneless hum. It joined with the birdsong, creating a kind of counterpoint. After a minute or so, Sing joined in with a lyric of her own and the music mounted. It was a crazy kind of music. But I guess that is just the way of things. The way of all living things in this great gig of creation. Some crazy, pulsing unfinished song. And you have to listen closely to hear it but once you do all that is left for you is to get up and dance.

And so we did.